Celtic

Mythology

For Kids

A Comprehensive Guide to Learn All about the
Realms of Celtic Mythology from A-Z

URSULA SMITH

Table of Contents

Introduction

As our children grow older, it becomes essential for parents to engage them in legends about their culture and beliefs. Mythology is a significant part of any culture. It explains how our ancestors perceived and understood the world and what they celebrated in their rituals and traditions, some of which are still followed by the community. Folktales serve as the foundation of a community's way of thinking and operation. They teach our children and us why we hold certain beliefs and celebrate specific festivals throughout the year.

Most legends are based on important life lessons and highlight the difference between good and evil deeds, making them an interesting learning opportunity for children. Not to mention that reading them will awaken your child's imagination, especially considering that Celtic mythology offers insight into a world of deities, fairies, and witches. Reading these tales will heighten their curiosity and make them keen to explore the world around them.

Celtic mythology originated from numerous regions and tribes. Most of the stories come from Island and Wales, while others come from Scotland, Cornwall, and Brittany. Celtic mythology can be divided into four groups, commonly known as cycles. The first one explains how deities and other mystical beings first settled in

Ireland. The second cycle mainly focuses on the theme of hunting. This cycle features stories about the protection of the Scottish and Irish lands. The third one revolves around themes like warfare and victory as it tells the story of the Ulaidh tribe. Last but not least, the last cycle, known as the Kings Cycle, gathers a set of compelling stories based on real kings in history.

Celtic mythology is characterized by its fascinating themes of magic, heroic endeavors, romance, and mystical adventure. These tales have survived for millennia and have remained relevant despite foreign invasions and influences, showing how strongly rooted they are. Celts believed in the existence of the Otherworld, which is a realm that inhabits the deities and other supernatural beings. According to some beliefs, this world also housed the dead. In most cases, the Celtic Otherworld is known for being a place of eternal youth, beauty, and joy.

This book takes its readers through the entire journey of Celtic mythology. It explores how the gods landed in Ireland and ended up in the Otherworld and guide readers through the incredible stories of Cu Chulainn, the children of Lir, Conaire Mor, and other significant figures in mythology. As you read on, you will learn how Earth and the other realms are depicted in lore. You will also learn about the countless peoples mentioned in the cycles and the most fantastical creatures of Celtic mythology.

Special events are also covered in great detail, such as The Cattle Raid of Cooley. It also delves deep into Tir Na N-Óg, the Irish Otherworld, and illustrates the tales in this wondrous realm.

This book serves as a comprehensive guide to the world of Celtic mythology. It is very educational, easy to read, and incredibly interesting. Even though it's written especially for children, many adults can also benefit from reading it.

Chapter 1

The Celtic Gods and Goddesses

You are probably familiar with names like Thor, Loki, and Odin, especially if you are a Marvel fan. Let's be honest, who isn't? You know that these awesome Marvel heroes are gods, right? You may not know that Marvel didn't create these three characters, Thor, Loki, and Odin; they are originally a part of Norse mythology.

History is filled with fascinating gods and goddesses that will make you rethink and battle to choose your favorite one. This chapter will talk about many interesting Celtic gods and goddesses who are even more powerful than your favorite superheroes.

Dagda

There is no better god to start discovering than Dagda since he was the most powerful Celtic deity. He is known as An Dagda, which means "The Good God," but no one knows the origin of his name. Dagda is the creator of life and is often regarded as a father figure. He is usually compared to another great god, Odin, Thor's father, but unlike the Odin we see in the movies, Dagda is a very friendly, cheerful, and fun god.

- **Origins and Associations**

  There once was a tribe of supernatural beings and gods called the Tuatha Dé Danann that lived in the Otherworld, which is like a parallel universe where gods lived, and other mythical heroes could visit. Dagda was their king and leader, which explains his immense power. He wasn't just a father in name, but he acted like one as well. He protected all beings, which is why he is usually compared to Odin. However, he shares some similarities with Thor as well. Both are strong warriors with powerful weapons, but instead of a hammer, our Celtic god had a club called "lorg mór."

  Dagda went by various names like "Ruad Rofhessa," which means the "Mighty one of great knowledge," and "Eochaid

Ollathair," which means" great father." His father was Elatha, the king of the Fomorians. Ogma, the God of speech, and Lir, the sea God, were his brothers. He is one of the most important gods in Celtic mythology since he played a huge role when Ireland was invaded.

Way back in history, a group of people called the Milesians invaded Ireland; they fought with the Tuatha Dé Danann and drove them underground. Dagda then decided to split the tribe's lands among himself and other gods.

He was also considered the god of knowledge, and the Druids have gained their magic and wisdom from him.

Dagda is associated with knowledge, wisdom, strength, agriculture, and weather. He is also highly respected by the Druids since he was associated with their magic as well.

- **Powers and Abilities**

Dagda could control life and death by using his club, which could take and restore life. Being the Tuatha Dé Danann king came with its perks, as Dagda owned one of its treasures, the "Daur da Bláo," a harp he used to control men's feelings and the seasons. He also had a magical cauldron that is said to be bottomless and never run out of food.

- **Physical Appearance**

Dagda looked nothing like the Roman, Greek, or Norse gods that we often see in pictures. He wasn't fit or had six-packs. In fact, this joyful god was a chubby, large, and bearded old man who fitted his father figure status. He was often shown wearing a rustic tunic, holding his club in one hand and carrying the cauldron over his shoulder.

- **Family and Relationships**

Dagda fell in love with the river goddess Boann, and they had a son named Óengus (also spelled Aengus), who became the god of love. When she was pregnant, he used his powers to stop the sun from setting for nine whole months. So technically, his son was born in one day. He also fell in love with the goddess of war and fate, Morrigan. He is also the father of Brigid, the goddess of healers and poets, Bodb Derg, who became the king of the Tuatha Dé Danann after his father, and Midir, the creator of lakes and rivers in Ireland.

The Morrigan

The Morrigan is a very mysterious Deity, and she is the goddess of Fate, battle, and war. She has various names like Morrígu, Morríghan, and Mor-Ríoghain, Irish for "phantom queen."

If you think that Morrigan's name sounds familiar or that she reminds you of a certain legend, you are correct. She is often linked to Morgan Le Fay from the legend of Arthur and Merlin. However, some people say the only connection they share is in the sounds of their names, but if you watch the TV show, Merlin, you may see some similarities.

- **Origins and Associations**

The Morrigan is associated with war, battle, sovereignty, and land. She is also associated with other war gods like Nemain and Macha.

According to legend, Morrigan fell in love with a very powerful warrior called Cu Chulainn, but he didn't feel the same way. Ouch! Unfortunately for this mighty warrior, our war goddess didn't take rejection very well. She used her shapeshifting ability to transform into different beings to attack him, but he managed to temporarily blind her in one eye, but don't worry, she tricked Cu Chulainn into healing her. So, what happened to this mighty warrior? Well, we won't spoil his story for you since it is discussed in the coming chapter.

She also aided her lover Dagda in one of his battles, where he emerged victoriously.

- **Powers and Abilities**

The Morrigan could shapeshift and take whatever form she desired. She mainly took the form of a crow which usually meant bad luck. She would also appear in her crow form on the battlefield to stir up the war mania in soldiers. In other legends, she would hover over battlefields to instill bravery in soldiers and frighten their opponents.

You may think that Morrigan enjoys bringing doom or chaos. However, she was also considered a guardian of the land and its people.

Since she is the Goddess of battle, she is the only one who decides which soldiers survive the battle; she can also predict how a battle will end.

- **Physical Description**

The Morrigan had red hair and often wore a red cloak. She can manifest as a crow or a raven, and in some legends, she takes the form of a wolf, a cow, an eel, a beautiful young woman, and an old woman as well.

- **Family and Relationships**

As mentioned, Morrigan was in love with Dagda. She was also romantically involved with Samhain. She was a member of the Tuatha Dé Danann as well.

Fun Fact - *The Samhain festival, which is still celebrated to this day in Ireland, is the inspiration behind Halloween.*

Lugh

Lugh is, also spelled as Lugus, Lug, or Lugos, is also considered one of the most important Celtic deities. He also had other names like Samildánach, which means "skilled in all arts," and Lugh Lámhfhada, which means "Lugh of the long arm." He was the sun god and is often compared to Mercury, the Roman god of merchants. He was also the god of talent, art, crafts, and skill. In some legends, he was a god of storms as well. He was one of the most famous members of the Tuatha Dé Danann.

- **Origins and Associations**

Lugh was a king and brave warrior and helped his tribe, the Tuatha Dé Danann, to victory against the Formorri, a race of hostile, supernatural beings, by killing their leader Balor. This resulted in making them the ruling tribe in Ireland.

He was associated with ravens, thunderstorms, and lynx, which are large wild cats.

- **Powers and Abilities**

Lugh was a skilled warrior and craftsman who often had a magical spear that flashed fire in battle. The spear had a mind of its own and a strong desire for fighting; it would even try to fight without Lugh.

When Lugh goes to battle, he often brings his invincible hound Fáil Inis with him. The hound has a really cool ability - as he can turn water into wine. Lugh is best described as someone who is good at everything, which is why he is considered one of the most powerful Celtic deities.

- **Physical Description**

According to legends, Lugh was a young and handsome warrior who wore a helmet and armor and held a spear called Gae Assail.

- **Family and Relationships**

Lugh was the son of Eithniu and Cian. His paternal grandmother was Danu, the mother of Earth. As mentioned,

Lugh killed Balor and was responsible for Formorii's loss. Interestingly, Balor was Lugh's grandfather from his mother's side Eithniu, making him a descendant of the Fomorii. This must have made family reunions pretty awkward. In fact, before Lugh was even born, a fortune teller had told Balor that his grandson would kill him.

Lugh married many women, including Nás, Buí, Englic, and Echtach. According to Celtic legends, Lugh was the divine father of the mighty warrior Cu Chulainn.

Fun Fact - *When there is a thunderstorm in Ireland, some people say that Balor and Lugh are fighting.*

Brigid

Brigid is also spelled Brigit and is the Goddess of healers, poetry, fire, fertility, and magicians. She has other names like Brigantia and Brighid. She was a triple Goddess with her sisters, also named Brigid, who all represented smithcraft, poetry, and healing. She is often compared to the Greek Goddess Athena.

- **Origins and Associations**

Brigid is associated with healing, childbirth, spring, and fertility. According to legend, the Goddess had so many animals like sheep, oxen, and boars. The animals didn't just serve as pets but were very useful as they would cry out to warn Brigid of any impending danger.

- **Powers and Abilities**

According to legend, Brigid protected women while they were giving birth. As a result, she became the Goddess of the hearth. She was also a healer and a protector of babies and their mothers. Brigid was also a muse who inspired poets and writers.

- **Physical Description**

Brigid is depicted as a young woman with red hair that resembles the color of fire. In various tales, she appears as a mother or maiden. She wore a cloak made of sunbeams.

- **Family and Relationships**

As mentioned, Brigid is the daughter of Dagda, which makes her a member of the Tuatha Dé Danann. She has two sisters who have the same name as hers. According to some legends, she married Bres, who was the ruler of Tuatha Dé Danann and had a son called Ruaden. In other legends, she married Tuireann, the god of thunder. They had three sons: Ircharba, Brian, and Luchar. It is believed that her three sons killed Lugh's father, Cian.

Cernunnos

Cernunnos is often referred to as the "Horned One" or the "Horned God" he is also the god of nature, animals, wealth, trees, and fertility. He is a very interesting and strange deity. He's usually shown as being around horned animals like bulls or stags, which he considered sacred. This is why he is referred to as " The Lord of Wild Things."

- **Origins and Associations**

Cernunnos is associated with nature, forest, horned animals, wealth, vegetation, and fertility. The Druids referred to him as the Honored god.

- **Powers and Abilities**

Cernunnos is a master hunter and a protector of the forest.

Other legends consider Cernunnos to be the god of death who would sing to the dead to calm their fears as they travel to the realm of the spirits.

- **Physical Description**

Cernunnos is often portrayed with shaggy hair, a beard, and wearing a huge metal ring, torc, and a stag's antlers over his head.

- **Family and Relationships**

Cernunnos married Beltane, the goddess of the Spring, but he died six months later.

Danu

Although she is one of the most prominent deities in Celtic mythology, little is known about her. However, we can't talk about Celtic goddesses without mentioning Danu, who is the mother of the most famous Celtic tribe, the Tuatha Dé Danann. She went by various names like Annad, Anu, and Ana.

- **Origins and Associations**

Danu isn't a typical goddess - you could say she is a big deal. She is one of the oldest Celtic deities, and she is the divine mother of the Tuatha Dé Danann. In fact, Tuatha Dé Danann translates as the people of the goddess Danu. She is also considered the mother of Ireland as well.

Danu was associated with nature, prosperity, strength, wisdom, regeneration, and death.

- **Powers and Abilities**

Danu was the goddess of power and sovereignty. She was the source of power for many leaders, kings, and chiefs, and she would often give gifts to people who come from noble birth. She also bestows creativity and skills to her children, the people of the Tuatha Dé Danann. She was also a source of wisdom that she instilled in many gods. She is also connected to the fairies and the earth.

- **Physical Description**

Illustrations of Danu show her to be a beautiful mature woman.

- **Family and Relationships**

She was a member of the Tuatha Dé Danann since she was the daughter of its ruler Dagda. We believe that Danu has been married, but no one knows her husband's name.

Aengus

Aengus or Óengus is the god of love and youth whose name translates as "True Vigor."

- **Origins and Associations**

As mentioned earlier, Aengus was born in a day because his father stopped the sun from setting before he was born. According to legend, when Aengus grew up, his father gave him Brú na Bóinne, a place in Ireland, as a gift. However, some legends say that this wasn't a gift, but he actually tricked his father into taking it.

One night, Aengus dreamed of a girl called Caer Ibormeith and fell in love with her in the dream. On waking, he became adamant about finding her. He searched all over and finally found her. However, the path of true love is never easy. She was one of 150 girls who all transformed into swans. If he wanted to marry her, he must identify her as a swan.

True love conquered all, and Aegnus identified Caer Ibormeith, and they had their happy ending. After recognizing his love, they both flew away while singing a beautiful song. Anyone who heard this song would fall asleep for three days and three nights. This is how Aengus became the god of young lovers. According to other legends, Aengus transformed into a swan to be able to identify his love.

Aengus is associated with the valley of the River Boyne.

- **Powers and Abilities**

As the god of love, Aengus has the power to make people fall in love, and women also find him irresistible. However, he never used his powers for evil as he refused to entice Caer. It was his sweet personality and his affection that made her fall for him. Romance runs in this deity's blood as he was also the chief poet of the Tuatha Dé Danann. Since he was conceived in a day, Aegnus didn't age.

- **Physical Description**

Aengus was a very handsome and charming young man with a lively personality. He is also depicted with four birds flying around his head, representing love.

- **Family and Relationships**

Aengus is the son of Dagda and the river goddess Boann. He was married to his love Caer Ibormeith.

Ériu

Ériu was a member of the Tuatha Dé Danann, and she was considered the goddess of Ireland. Her name has been modernized to Erin or Éire.

- **Origins and Associations**

Ériu kept the Tuatha Dé Danann legacy alive when the Milesians defeated them as she and her sisters were the ones that welcomed them, and as a thank you, the Milesians named the country after her. Ireland was actually named after Ériu.

This makes Ériu associated with Ireland. In other legends, the sisters fought the Milesians, but when they realized that they would not win this war, they only desired one thing: their names to be remembered forever. Each sister climbed her favorite mountain waiting for the Milesians. When they reached Ireland, the sisters asked for the land to be named after them, a request that the Milesians granted.

- **Powers and Abilities**

Ériu and her sisters Fódla and Banba formed a feminine trinity, and they were considered sovereigns.

- **Physical Description**

According to various illustrations, Ériu was a beautiful young woman with long red hair and dressed in green.

- **Family and Relationships**

Her father was Delbáeth, the God-King, and her mother was Ernmas, who was the Mother goddess. Both were considered the parents of the Tuatha Dé Danann. She had two sisters, Fódla and Banba. It is believed that she was married to Dagda's grandson, Mac Gréin, and her sisters also married two of Dagda's grandsons. However, according to other legends, she was in a relationship with Lugh, while other stories specify that she was in love with Elatha, who was a Fomorian prince, and they had a son called Bres. This must have been a forbidden love like Romeo and Juliet since the Tuatha Dé Danann and the Fomorians were enemies.

The world of Celtic gods is filled with magic, mystery, and adventure. It is so easy to get immersed in these beautiful stories. Unfortunately, these gods aren't as popular as the Romans and Greeks deities. However, you can see they are still fascinating. The Celts had gods for everything, whether it was love, youth, rivers, or storms. Each god has a story that humanizes them, like falling in love or becoming brave warriors. Come to think of it, these Deities aren't really so different from us—Magic and being powerful gods aside, of course.

Chapter 2

Mystical Places, Their Peoples and Legendary Creatures

The history of the world is rich and extensive. You may be surprised to learn that most of what we know about it, especially the portion of history that goes all the way back before people started keeping written records, comes from legend and folktales. Folklore, legend, and myth are deeply intertwined with the way that we understand various cultures and histories of the world. These stories impact our perception and understanding of the world's past, present, and future. Similarly, our ancestors initially came up with those tales because it was their way of making sense of the world. Storytelling helped them understand concepts like virtue, morals, righteousness, human behavior, and the nature of life.

Myths are typically tales that revolve around gods, goddesses, and other divine figures. They are intended to answer profound questions about the universe, such as how the world was created, where and how the gods originated, where humans come from, and how people learned basic life skills like metal-smithing and making fires. The word "myth" is usually used to refer to one aspect of a very long story. If you're familiar with the Irish pantheon of the gods and the Four Branches of the Mabingoni, you have a very good idea of what a typical myth looks like. "Origin mythology" is one very popular type of myth, and it refers to tales that discuss where a certain group of people came from.

Legends mainly revolve around distinct heroes. The myth may depict their legendary figures as regular human beings or grant them superhuman qualities depending on the culture. Most legends are very closely linked to certain places. The significance of these locations may be based on prominent wars, the birthplace of a hero, or similar events. Folklore can be linked to deeply held cultural beliefs. These include the role and general existence of mystical creatures like fairies, rituals, and more.

Why Do They Matter?

Myths and legends are shared globally because they reflect the essence of human experience at their core. The cycles of nature, human physical, mental and psychological traits, and the general course of life, including birth, unions, marriage, pregnancy, childbearing, aging, and death, make great topics and inevitably give rise to very interesting tales. Myths often revolve around finding or losing love, parenting, all its challenges, and even pointless efforts to vanquish the space between the physical and spiritual realms or the concepts of life and death. Among other topics of importance, these perils are relatable to all humans regardless of where they are located in the world.

Researchers are still not entirely sure about how myths, legends, and folklore are spread and modified from one location to the other. Natives pass down important pieces of lore from one generation to the next. These short stories serve a very important lesson: to communicate vital life lessons and pieces of information by organizing them into a memorable, understandable, and helpful form. The main purpose behind lore is to educate people, especially children, on why you can't wander deep into the forest or climb mountaintops all by yourself.

Cultural and traditional stories usually cover moral and ethical topics. They also give you a revelation about how people behave and think. These tales urge you to fulfill your promises, make mindful decisions, and promote determination and courage. Stories like these teach their readers that evil will never win. Unlike legends, those types of narratives don't always revolve around superhuman or vigorous and muscular heroic figures. Instead, the protagonist is often witty, smart, and cunning, taking the form of a child or a poor individual who can find a quick solution to a prevailing problem.

This chapter will explore Celtic mythology's most prominent mystical places and realms. We will also discuss the main Celtic peoples and legendary creatures and their prominence in Celtic society.

Realms and the Otherworld

The idea of a mystical Otherworld is very widespread and found in various myths. This concept has been prevalent among numerous cultural groups since the beginning of time. The ancient Celts believed that their deities inhabited the Otherworld. It was also thought that this realm was that of the dead and other mystical creatures like Twylyth Teg and fairies. Some stories tell of how those who live in this realm can enjoy an eternity of good health, beauty, happiness, youth, and abundance. Many believed that those who move onto the Otherworld get to have all their needs fulfilled.

According to Celtic beliefs, you can't easily enter the Otherworld because it's concealed and hard to locate. However, with enough perseverance and dedication, some people manage to find it. Ancient Celts also thought people could be escorted, invited, or guided toward the Otherworld. Other methods to get to the

Otherworld included burial mounds or the crossing of water bodies. Some special caves, lakes, burial mounds, bogs, and hills were popularly thought to grant access to the spiritual world.

Another popular belief suggests that the Otherworld exists in an alternate reality or dimension. It was thought to be somewhat like a mirror world. The barriers that separated the earthly and spiritual realms were believed to become weaker and thinner during Samhain and Beltane, making it easier to transport and communicate between both worlds. The following are two of the most popular examples of Celtic Otherworlds:

- **Annwn**

Annwn is the Otherworld of Celtic Welsh mythology. To the Welsh, the Otherworld was an entirely different realm with its own boundaries and limitations. Many folktales featured huntsmen being led into Annwn by a deer or stag.

In *Pwyll, Prince of Dyfed*, the tale of the First Branch of the Mabinogi, Pwyll's hunting activities infuriated Arawn, the King of the Otherworld. Hoping to ease his anger, Pwyll agreed to exchange bodies with Arawn and spend one day as the king killing Hafgan, his enemy. Hafgan was also the King of Annwn, suggesting the existence of multiple Otherworlds. Arawn invited Pwyll to access the Otherworld and escorted him to his palace in Annwn. There, he succeeded in killing Hafgan and married Rhiannon, a beautiful goddess.

- **Oisin in Tír na nÓg**

There are numerous ways to refer to the Otherworld of Irish mythology. However, "the Land of the Youth," known as "Tír na nÓg" in Irish, is the most popular term. The story of Oisin provides a great deal of insight into life in this Otherworld. This tale is very similar to the story of Pwyll mentioned above.

Oisin, who was hunting deer, was guided to the Otherworld by Niamh. Like Rhiannon, Niamh is exceptionally beautiful and rides a magical white horse. The protagonist and the goddess arrive at the Land of the Youth on the back of the horse that gallops on the water's surface. Even though the inhabitants of Tír na nÓg were granted everything they wished for, Oisin preferred to get things done himself. This is why he sought the excitement of hunting. Unfortunately, the hero found that all his hunts ended perfectly, and this lacked the excitement and authenticity of real hunting activities.

Naturally, he got bored and wished for more suspense and exhilaration in his life. While this was granted, Oisin was never in real danger. He decided that he wanted to go back to his regular life, which is a wish that Niamh hesitatingly agreed to. While he thought his visit to the Otherworld was short, it actually lasted for centuries in the physical realm. He returned to find that all his friends and family were dead.

Immortal Settlers

Celtic immortal settlers share human-like features and emotions, such as weaknesses, greed, anger, strength, and beauty. Many are characterized by their shape-shifting abilities and their deep association with nature. The following are some of the most important settlers:

- **Tuatha de Danann (And Their Four Treasures)**

The Tuatha de Danann are divine people who arrived in Ireland after obtaining indispensable knowledge and skills. It's said that they landed in clouds of mist. They came bearing Four Treasures that they had obtained from Findias, Gorias, Murias, and Falias, which are four mystical cities. Each of the treasures is named after a significant deity.

- **The Sword of Nuada**

The sword of Nuada comes from Findias. When this weapon is pointed toward a specific target, it leaves them unable to move. They are also forced to provide a truthful answer to any question they're asked. They can also identify any forms of deception and gain a heightened sense of self-awareness and responsibility. Lastly, whoever held the sword could not be beaten in a fight.

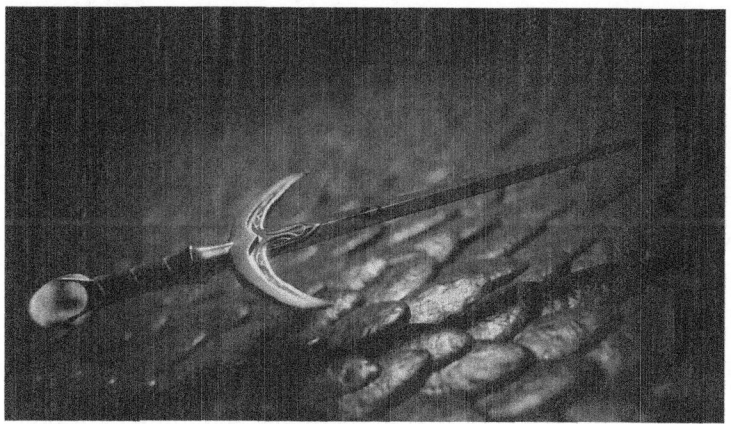

- **The Spear of Lugh**

This treasure comes from Gorias and is unbeatable. Its bearer can never be defeated and is given the powers of persuasive and charismatic qualities. The powers of victory, determination, and persistence lie in the spear.

- **Undry- The Dagda's Cauldron**

The Dagda's Cauldron comes from Murias. This cauldron leaves everyone fulfilled and satisfied. It's a symbol of abundance, regeneration, and restoration. Undry is also highly nurturing and is representative of generosity.

- **The Lia Fáil**

The Lia Fáil is believed to be the Stone of Destiny and can be found on the mound of Tara. This treasure imitates a crying noise when a rightful monarch touches it. This stone is believed to be a symbol of tradition, sovereignty, nature, and integrity.

• Fomorians

Fomorians are believed to be Ireland's first settlers. They inhabited Ireland two centuries before the Partholons arrived to overthrow them. However, the Partholons died of the plague, and the remaining Fomorians were met with the people of Nemed.

This semi-divine race was depicted as an evil spirit that lived underwater and in other underground locations by many. Others, however, portrayed them as sea raiders. Some tales describe them to possess the head of a goat and the body of a man or as creatures that have only one eye, arm, and leg. While both of these depictions are horrendous, some figures, like Bres and Elatha, his father, were thought to be rather beautiful. Fomorians are believed to be the descendants of the people who settled in Canaan and who were forced to leave their lands.

• Fir Bolg

A great number of the Irish population is thought to be made up of people who stayed behind after numerous invasions from a wide range of peoples. The Fir Blogs are said to be the fourth group of invaders and the descendants of the third invading peoples: the Muintir Nemid. The Greeks had enslaved the Fir Bolg for over two centuries. However, much to the Greek's worry, the Fir Bolg were growing in numbers. They were now able to come up with a solid escape plan, which the five brothers primarily devised. Before they left off, they decided to divide Ireland into five pieces of land so each brother could rule over a region. They named Sláine mac Dela (one of the brothers) chieftain, who was, in turn, Ireland's first High King. The Fir Bolgs were driven out of Ireland by the Tuatha de Danann.

- **Milesians**

The divine race that kicked the Tuatha De Danann out of Ireland and underground was known as the Milesians. They are among the Celtic population's most notable ancestors because it's believed that they came bearing proof that the land was rightfully theirs. Medieval Irish historians suggested that the gods were driven out of the surface into the land and into the ancient burial mounds. As we mentioned above, the burial mounds were thought to be pathways to the Otherworld, where they would continue to live.

- **Fairies**

The Tuatha De Danann are also thought to be the fairies. Fairies were generally mystical, mysterious, and highly secretive. The Milesians and other strong tribes fought with the Tuatha De Danann and defeated them upon their arrival to Ireland. However, they never forced them out. Because they loved Ireland profoundly, the Tuatha De Danann decided to shrink themselves using their magical powers so they could live underground. People say that there are tunnels beneath the grounds of Ireland that travel all across the nation, leading to various villages of fairies. According to myth, each fairy village is said to be marked by a nearby Lone Bush or hawthorn tree.

Local Irish peoples typically blame the fairies for natural phenomena that they don't understand. This is why the fairies don't like to interact with people and wish to be left alone. For this reason, disturbing a Lone Bush or single hawthorn tree is believed to bring bad luck.

- **Fianna**

The Fianna were a ferocious group of warriors who moved around the land of Ireland. Their tales make up Irish mythology's Finian Cycle. The Fianna included notable figures throughout the years, like Oisin and Fionn Mac Cumhaill, who was the last Fian leader. His wit and intelligence characterized this legendary figure. At some point, he was thought to be the most knowledgeable man in the entire Irish nation. His wisdom granted him the ability to easily take on a much larger and stronger enemy and win in the process.

Legendary Creatures

- **Balor**

Balor, who was known as the Balor of the Evil Eye, was the leader of all Fomorians. He is considered a mystical Celtic demon. As you can gather from the name, the creature was one large-eyed giant. One day, Balor decided to sneak up on his father's Druids. To his bad luck, they were making spells out of which troubling vapors escaped and went right into his eye. As a result, Balor was left with a swollen eye that gave him the power of death.

- **Donn Cuailnge**

Donn Cuailnge is Irish myth's greatest, largest, and most vicious bully. It used to promenade the Cooley Peninsula's great forests and greenery. If you are familiar with the Cattle Raid of Cooley, which is one of the most well-known battles in Celtic and Irish mythology, you probably already know of this legendary bull.

- **Banshee**

Garnering a lot of popularity in pop culture, the Banshee is among the most famous mythological creatures in Irish mythology. This legendary figure is also easily recognizable due to the prevalence of storytelling and sharing in Irish culture. The Banshee is a Celtic female spirit that takes the form of numerous entities. For instance, she is often depicted as an old woman with rather scary eyes, a pale woman who wears a white dress, and even a pretty lady in a shroud. However, the Banshee is not known for her alternating looks and many appearances, but she is known for her irksome shrieks and wails. This legendary figure voices her prophecies of impending doom.

- **The Dullahan**

Those who know very little about Irish mythology and the origins of fairies view them as wholesome little mythological creatures. Fairies are very popular in pop culture and among little kids, and they are typically portrayed as beautiful beings with a plethora of mythical powers. However, the Dullahan destroys all these common misconceptions, as this portrayal of a fairy is nothing but happy and cute. The Dullahan is a headless fairy that rides on the back of a black horse, and legend says that the Dullahan uses a human spine for a whip and can prophesy deaths. If he calls out a person's name, they die right at that moment.

- **The Cailleach**

The Cailleach appears in many forms. Her appearance largely depends on the story and the person telling it. According to ancient Irish folktales, this mythological creature was believed to be a hag. It was said that she was the mastermind behind the creation of planet Earth. Scottish legends, however, portray her as a creature with the incredible ability to influence and alter the weather. For this reason, many people refer to the Cailleach as the Queen of the Winter. She is considered among the most prominent Celtic mythological figures. Additionally, many Irish poets found inspiration in her wind and weather-controlling powers.

- **Aibell**

Aibell is one of many Irish legendary figures that have used music to bring their enemies to their demise. So, what's unique about this creature? She also happens to be the guardian of an Irish clan known as the Dál gCais. Additionally, she is the Fairy Queen of Thomond. Aibell inhabited the lands of Craig Liath and played her magic harp beautifully. Tragically, those who listened to her play would die.

- **Aos Sí**

Aos Sí can be translated into "people of the mound." These Irish mythological creatures are highly protective. They also take numerous forms and can appear to be either deformed or beautiful. Legend says that people who offend the people of the mound would be subject to agonizing revenge.

While each country has its own extensive collection of native myths and legends, the general synopsis of these tales is unexpectedly pervasive across the globe. This means that many storylines are shared universally with varying characters and details. Did you know that you can find versions of Cinderella, Kind Arthur, and other stories in different parts of the world? The main reason behind this phenomenon is that these tales were essentially exchanged through trade, intercultural marriages, conquests, and migration. These tales are also passed down from one generation to the other. In countries where the sense of culture is deep-rooted, people still exchange folktales and legends to this day.

Chapter 3

How the Gods Came to Ireland

Now that you have familiarized yourself with the Celtic gods and goddesses, you probably have one question on your mind - how did it all start? How did the gods come to Ireland?

Celtic myths can be divided into four cycles, and together they tell the story of how Ireland came to be. Each one of these cycles is filled with adventures, battles, and great stories of gods, kings, and heroes.

The Mythological Cycle

The first cycle is the mythological cycle, and it took place before the arrival of Christianity. As is obvious from the name, it focuses on Celtic legends and myths. It tells the story of the Tuatha Dé Dannan, who we have talked about in previous chapters; remember them? This cycle is about their arrival in Ireland and their eventual disappearance underground. Their disappearance paved the way for the Aos Sí, another group of supernatural beings, to rise and rule Ireland. They are the Irish mythological creatures, many of which you are familiar with, like the leprechauns or the Merrow.

The Ulster Cycle

Back in history, northern Leinster and eastern Ulster were two of Ireland's biggest and most well-known cities. The two cities were called Ulaid; The Ulster cycle is named after one of the cities, Ulster. This cycle started after the birth of Jesus Christ in the first century. However, some believe that many tales took place before Christianity, specifically during the Medieval period. It features many heroic tales and quests which took place in the Ulaid.

The Fenian Cycle

The Fenian Cycle is the third cycle and is often confused with the Ulster cycle. During this cycle, warriors were so popular that people worshiped them. The Fenian Cycle revolves around the heroic tales of mighty warriors, including their love stories as well.

The cycle also features the incredible journey of Fionn Mac Cumhail with his powerful army. We will talk about the fascinating adventures of Fionn in the next chapter.

The Historical or Kings Cycle

The last cycle is the Historical cycle which mainly focuses on Medieval royalty. The stories are passed down to us from the point of view of the kings' poets.

Every story has a beginning, and these legends began with fascinating tales of battles and heroes. The stories that we will discuss in this chapter are all from the Mythological Cycle. However, we will discuss stories from the other cycles in the coming chapters.

The First Battle of Magh Tuireadh

You probably saw the title and thought, "the first battle"? Yes, two epic battles were fought by the Tuatha Dé Dannan at the Magh Tuireadh. The first one was against the fourth invaders of Ireland, the Fir Bolg.

The Fir Bolg ruled Ireland for thirty-seven years. Although this wasn't a long time, to this day, the people of Ireland tell stories of their fair king Eochaid mac Eirc. So why did the Fir Bolg only rule the country for a short time? One day, a group of people called the Tuatha Dé Dannan unexpectedly arrived in Ireland. You are familiar with them by now, but the people of Fir Bolg weren't since they know nothing about them or their origins. They basically came from nowhere and decided to make Ireland their new home.

At the time, the Tuatha Dé Dannan king was called Nuada, and he asked Eochaid mac Eirc for half of the island. The Fir Bolg's king refused to give up their land, so did the Tuatha Dé Dannan say thank you and leave? We guess you already know the answer to that. This is how the First Battle of Magh Tuireadh started, and it wasn't just about half of the island anymore.

Both groups were fighting over the whole land. The battle lasted for four days. Since this is a story about gods and heroes, we have to expect a heroic act, right? Fir Bolg had a champion who was called Sreng; this fierce warrior challenged the Tuatha Dé Dannan king to single combat. Nuada agreed, and both faced each other. The victory was for the warrior Sreng, who cut the king's arm off. However, this victory didn't matter at all. The Tuatha Dé Dannan defeated the Fir Bolg's army; even their king was killed by the Morrigan.

The victorious Tuatha Dé Dannan became the ruler of Ireland, so what happened to the Fir Bolg? Well, there are two different stories here. According to one legend, Tuatha Dé Danann was impressed by the courage of the Fir Bolg's soldiers, who, with a few soldiers left, vowed to fight to the last man and gave them a quarter of the country, which was Connaught. The other story claims that the Tuatha Dé Dannan didn't win the battle, but both parties decided to reach an agreement and split the country between them. The Fir Bolg only got a small portion, though, which was Connaught.

However, a different story suggests that after the Firbolgs were defeated, they fled Ireland.

We imagine the Fir Bolg king wished he could go back in time and give the Tuatha Dé Danann half the land to spare himself this headache.

So, who ruled the Firbolgs after their king died? After the passing of the Fir Bolg's king, it is believed that the people chose Sreng to be their new leader. So, his amazing courage was rewarded.

Although the arrival of the Tuatha Dé Dannan was a surprise to the Firbolgs, it wasn't for their king Eochaid. Legend says that Eochaid dreamt that a fleet of ships arrived in Ireland. Back then, people didn't make their dreams lightly, and there were many interpreters of dreams. When the king told his poet about what he dreamed, he warned him that this was a prophecy.

Now back to the Tuatha Dé Danann, what happened to their king after his arm was cut off?

King Nuada and His Severed Arm

Nuada wasn't only a king but was also the god of hunting and fishing. He was one of the most skilled hunters Tuatha Dé Danna had seen. He was also an intelligent and sensible king who respected everyone. His laws were fair, and his generosity knew no bounds. In fact, his laws were applied to everyone, even himself.

As mentioned, during the first battle of the Magh Tuireadh, Nuada lost his arm. According to some legends, the king asked Sreng to tie his own arm to make it a fair fight, but the Fir Bolg champion refused. This led the Tuatha Dé Danann to offer Connaught to the Fir Bolg to save their king.

Although the first battle of the Magh Tuireadh ended with the victory of the Tuatha Dé Danann, their king Nuada wasn't so victorious. He didn't only lose his arm, but he also lost the throne. The Tuatha Dé Danna law that Nuada had created stated that their king must be in perfect shape to rule. Now that Nuada had lost his arm, he didn't seem fit to lead the Tuatha Dé Danna and had no choice but to abdicate. He chose Bres to take his place, a choice that proved to be a big mistake.

However, this wasn't the end of Nuada, as Bre's rule didn't last long, luckily for the people of the Tuatha Dé Danna. A silver arm was crafted for Nuada by his physician Dian Cécht, the God of healing and the son of Dagda. It was a long and hard operation that took nine days, but it was all worth it since it made Nuada whole again and fit to be king. This is why Nuada is referred to as Nuada of the Silver arm in many tales. Bres's rule only lasted for seven years which is a good thing, and you will find out why in the next part.

The Reign of Bres

As mentioned in a previous chapter, Bres was the son of Ériu, a member of the Tuatha Dé Danna, and Elatha, a Fomorian, so basically, Bres was half Fomorian. As you know by now, they were enemies of the Tuatha Dé Danna. So, you can see why choosing him as a king was a mistake.

Bres was proof that beauty isn't everything because he was very good-looking, but he had an ugly personality. He got his looks from his mother since the Fomorians were monstrous in looks and personality. So why did Nuada choose Bres, knowing he was half Fomorians? It is believed that Bres was chosen as an olive branch to help bring peace between the two races. However, this wasn't achieved because Bres was simply a jerk.

Unlike his predecessor, Bres was an unjust king who oppressed his subjects. He was a coward and favored the Fomorians and conspired with them against his people. He made the Tuatha Dé Danna pay taxes and allowed them to be enslaved by the Fomorians. Deities like Dagda, the god of wisdom, and Oghma, the god of knowledge and a poet, were humiliated and enslaved.

However, the people grew frustrated and couldn't handle the oppression. So how do oppressed people express themselves? Through art, music, or - in this case, poetry. A poet called Cairbre mac Éadoine spoke up by satirizing Bres. The people, encouraged by the satire to speak up, demanded Bres give up the throne. However, he was allowed to remain a king until he served seven years, which he used to torment the Tuatha Dé Danna with the help of the Fomorians.

Bres loved being a king and didn't want to give up the throne. However, when the seven years were up, and Nuada became whole again, he came back for his throne and became king of the Tuatha Dé Danna for a second time. We wish we could tell you that all went well after Nuada took back his throne, but this wasn't the case. Bres was bitter, and the Fomorians were more ruthless than ever.

The Fall of Bres and the Rise of Lugh

After Nuada became king, Bres was really bitter. He first sought his father's help, but he was turned down. Although Elatha was a Fomorian, he didn't agree with the way his son ruled the Tuatha Dé Danna and was actually ashamed of him. We guess not all the Fomorians are bad. Bres had to seek help elsewhere, so who better to help him than the people he sided with and betrayed the gods of the Tuatha Dé Danna for?

Bres went to the ruler of the Fomorians, a giant and strong supernatural being called Balor, and asked for his help. Both agreed it was the right time to wage war against the Tuatha Dé Danna. This was when the second battle of the Magh Tuireadh took place, that we will discuss next.

Bres led the Fomorian army, and Nuada appointed lugh to lead the Tuatha Dé Danna army. In a previous chapter, we mentioned that Lugh was the sun god and the god of skill and crafts. He was a mighty warrior and the perfect choice to lead Nuada's army. Balor was Lugh's maternal grandfather who made Lugh part Fomorian like Bres. However, unlike Bres, Lugh was loyal to the Tuatha Dé Danna and determined to go against his grandfather for the sake of his people. Going against his grandfather wasn't a hard decision for Lugh since Balor ordered to have him drowned when he was born; remember why? Take a look at the first chapter to refresh your memory.

41

Baby Lugh survived, thanks to a Druid woman who cast a spell that saved him and brought him to his Tuatha Dé Danna father, Cian. Lugh was raised with his people, who trained him to be a great warrior and made him fit to lead their army years later. When Lugh grew up, he wished to join the king's household. However, this wasn't an easy task. They were looking for people, or in this case gods, with special and different skills.

Each skill Lugh told them he possessed; he was told they already had someone with this skill. Lugh didn't have just one skill; he had many, which he used to make his case. He argued that they might have each skill, but they don't have someone who possessed all of them, like being a smith, harper, poet, a magician, a warrior, champion, and a physician. That convinced the king's doorman, and Lugh was allowed to join Nuada's household. Lugh proved himself in the king's court by playing the harp, competing against the flagstone throwing champion Ogma in a contest, and winning. During this time, the Fomorians were oppressing the Tuatha Dé Danna, and Lugh couldn't understand how the Tuatha Dé Danna was ok with this treatment.

Lugh had it all, the skill, the heart, the courage, and the personality to lead the Tuatha Dé Danna army. He wanted to free his people from the oppression of the Fomorians; Nuada saw this and realized that he was the perfect choice to lead his army. According to some legends, Nuada actually knew of the prophecy that Balor would die at the hands of his grandson, and he knew that Lugh was Barlor's grandson. It is believed that this was why he let Lugh lead his army. Either way, it was a good decision.

Lugh led the Tuatha Dé Danna, and Bres led the Fomorians. One was driven by the hope to free his people from oppression, while the other was driven by envy, anger, and vengeance. One rose and became a king while the other fell and lost it all.

The Second Battle of Magh Tuireadh

The second battle of the Magh Tuireadh was between the Tuatha Dé Danna and the Fomorians. After years of preparing for war, the two armies finally faced each other. With so much history between the two races, the battle was fierce. Balor and Nuada battled each other, but unfortunately, the brave king of the Tuatha Dé Danna was killed at the hands of Balor. The Tuatha Dé Danna army felt discouraged when they lost their king. Suddenly, things changed, and the soldiers had hope and felt encouraged to keep fighting and win. It was the screams of the Morrigan who shapeshifted into a crow and restored their courage so that they could defeat their enemy.

Lugh was angry that his king suffered such a terrible fate and decided to avenge Nuada. Lugh and Balor fought each other, the grandfather and the grandson. The prophecy was fulfilled, and Balor died at the hands of his grandson. Balor was gone, the Fomorian army was devastated, and the Tuatha Dé Danann won the second battle of the Magh Tuireadh.

Now that Nuada was dead, Lugh became the ruler of the Tuatha Dé Danna. On the other hand, Bres had now lost everything: his grandfather, who supported him, was gone, his army perished, and he was left alone and unprotected. He begged Lugh and the Tuatha Dé Danna to spare his life and promised them to use his powers to guarantee that all the cows in Ireland would always produce milk, but his offer was rejected. He promised that he would provide them with four harvests every year, which was also rejected. However, Lugh agreed to spare his life on one condition, which was to help the Tuatha Dé Danna by giving them agriculture tips.

Lugh ruled the Tuatha Dé Danna, and he was more like Nuada than Bres. He was a fair, wise, and brave king. Instead of using his Fermornin blood to betray his people and wage wars like Bres, he used it to bring peace between the two races. Lugh remained king for forty years which brought prosperity to his people, and the land thrived under his rule.

Both Bres and Lugh had the same circumstances; they were both half Fomorians and were chosen to be kings during unfortunate circumstances. Bres chose the dark side, and instead of bringing peace between his people, he chose betrayal and siding with the

Formians to destroy the Tuatha Dé Danna. He could have achieved peace and spared so much blood on both sides, but he let his anger and bitterness at being overthrown control him, unlike Lugh, who took advantage of his position to bring peace and become a just ruler. He was the bigger person and spared Bres's life; Bres would have never made this choice if the tables had been turned.

Although these legends are fun and interesting to read, there is always a moral lesson. Life is all about choices. We can't blame our circumstances on making the wrong one or hurting other people. The stories of Lugh and Bres are the perfect example to show that being good or bad is all about choices. Lugh showed us that by making the choices, Bres was afraid to make. Being a just ruler and a good person requires bravery which was clear in the story of these heroic Gods. So always be brave enough to make the right choice and choose mercy when you are the one in power.

We can learn many things from the Celtic Gods, lessons to follow, and mistakes to avoid.

Chapter 4

The Many Adventures
of Finn McCool

There are many tales of heroes in Irish mythology, yet, only a few are as riveting as the adventures of Finn McCool. Known as Fionn mac Cumhaill by the Irish, he was destined to be a mighty warrior from the day he was born. During his life, he had many triumphs and learned many lessons. These made him wise and very popular among bards, poets, and the older generation of Celts, who would spend their days telling tales about Finn McCool. This chapter contains some of the most famous adventures this hero went on as he grew from a young boy to the leader of the Fianna.

Finn and the Fianna

The Fianna were an ancient group of warriors many feared. They guarded Conn of the Hundred Battles, also known as the High King of Ireland. When they weren't at the battle, defending their ruler, the Fianna lived in large groups, often gathering on cold winter nights to listen to the tales of the old and wise. They trained, worked the fields, and slept under the open sky during summer. They were also avid hunters, often raiding the rich forests of Ireland. The Fianna hunted on horseback and were often accompanied by their faithful wolfhounds. According to legend, the hounds stood as tall as a horse, were fast on their feet, and with their keen sense of smell, they could track down any creature in the forest.

One of the leaders of the Fianna was Cumhall, Finn McCool's father. When his father lost the battle against Goll mac Morna, Finn's mother Muirne sent him to live with the warriors Bodhmall and Liath Luachra. They taught him so many skills that by the time he was ten, Finn already knew all the ways of the wild. Legend has it he could take down his prey with a single cast of a slingshot stone or a single swing of a sword. He could run as fast as a deer and learned to track wild animals with the help of hounds.

When he was fourteen, Finn decided that he would become the leader of the Fionna one day, just as his father had in his time. However, to do this, he still had to learn many things. One of these was poetry and the tales re-telling the ancient wisdom of the Celts. As he was looking for someone to teach him, he came across Finegas, a Druid who lived on the banks of the River Boyne. And this is where he had one of his greatest adventures - the encounter with the Salmon of Knowledge.

The Salmon of Knowledge

In Celtic Ireland, hazelnut trees were considered sacred and said to carry great wisdom. One of these magical trees was located on the bank of the River Boyne, where young Finn McCool lived with the poet Finegas. It's said that the salmon living in the River Boyne ate the nuts that fell into the river, inheriting its magical properties. This Salmons of Knowledge was coveted by many Druids who spent their lives dedicated to learning everything they could about the world. Since Finn asked him to teach him everything he needed to know about defeating his father's enemies,

Finegas took his task very seriously. He had spent years and years trying to catch the salmon, but the fish always eluded him. Finally, after seven years of trying, with the boy's help, Finegas successfully caught the Salmon of Knowledge. Both of them were so happy having the fish in their hands that when young Finn eagerly asked if he could cook it, Finegas agreed. He and all the other teachers taught Finn every skill and knowledge they possessed, but it wasn't enough, for the youngster still lacked the courage to take on the enemy. But now, Finegas could give him access to infinite wisdom.

Wanting the fish to taste the best, Finegas gave specific instructions on how to cook it. It's said that the Salmon of Knowledge had rainbow-colored scales, and the Druid didn't want to burn them. He instructed Finn to cook it over a slow-burning fire, turning it occasionally and pouring juices with herbs over both sides. He also told him to poke it with the small knife to ensure it was fully cooked, but he forbade Finn to taste it. After all, he wanted to be the first to gain access to its great wisdom. Finn thought this request was rather unusual. He was often instructed on how to cook meals - but he was always allowed to take small bites of the meals he cooked to ensure they were well done and flavored to Finegan's liking. He also wondered how Finegan would change after tasting the fish.

Still, guessing that the Salmon of Knowledge deserved special treatment, he obeyed - or, at least, tried to. He lit the fire and, when it was reduced to low flames, placed the fish over it, pouring the juices generously as he was instructed. As Finn was turning the fish, he accidentally touched its bubbling surface. After crying out in pain as he burnt his thumb on the salmon's hot skin, he put his finger into his mouth to soothe the ache. Suddenly, his mind was filled with the salmon's wisdom - and he instantly knew how to defeat his father's greatest enemy, Goll mac Morna. After realizing this, he became afraid that Finegas would get angry with him for disobeying the orders and send him away. Finn had grown to love the older man and didn't want to leave his side, nor did he want to look for any other teacher.

While he knew that Finn no longer needed him to teach him anything, Finegas was more curious than angry. He asked young Finn to describe what he saw when granted wisdom. Finn then started to tell him about all the wonderful pictures he saw in his mind. They were bits and pieces from all the different cultures of the world. Realizing the Salmon of Knowledge wasn't meant for him, he even encouraged Finn to eat the rest of the fish.

And this is how Finn McCool gained the knowledge that allowed him to avenge his father and become the leader of the Fionna. After eating the Salmon of Knowledge, Finn McCool became one of the greatest warriors of Ireland. He was capable of legendary deeds unrivaled by many. Legend has it that whenever Finn wanted to know more about what's happening around him - including events from the future, he only needed to suck his thumb to learn it. He always knew when and how the enemy planned to attack and how the battle ended. It also said that his thumb had healing properties, and whoever drank from his hands was instantly cured of all their ailments.

Aillen, the Fire Breathing Goblin

Finn knew that he couldn't join the ranks of the Fianna just yet because everyone who wanted to do so was asked to swear faith to Goll Mac Morna. Knowing he would have to break his oath, he went to the High King, who at the time was a wise man named Cormac. When Finn arrived at the court, the ruler and his followers were having a feast. Suddenly, everyone stopped what they were doing as they recognized Finn McCool from his bright-colored hair. He stood bravely in front of Cormac, declaring that he was the son of Cumhall and that he would like to join the High King's service. This was the first time he openly acknowledged this because up to that moment, he lived in secrecy, fearing Goll Mac Morna's revenge. Knowing that Cumhall was indeed a great warrior, Cormac proudly welcomed Finn McCool into his army. The feast resumed and even became merrier, with the hounds joining in, too!

Soon after Finn swore faith to the High King, he had a chance to prove his bravery, for Ireland was hunted by a mythical creature called Aillen, or the fire-breathing goblin. It was said that the goblin lurked in the forests, luring its victims by singing in an enchanting voice and playing the harp. According to another version of the story, the creature lived in the Otherworld alongside other ancestral spirits. It was once a member of the Tuatha Dé Danann. Unlike most of this supernatural tribe who became gods and heroes, the soul of Aillen was tormented by chaos and death, so he wanted to bring the same to the living. Around Samhain, when the veil between this world and the spiritual world became almost invisible, Aillen and many other spirits had the chance to cross it through the fairy mounds. Since this also marked the time of the ancient Celtic Harvest Fest, this meant that the creature often found many people together.

Naturally, the High King of Ireland also often organized large gatherings, hosting other kings and all the nobility from his kingdom. However, every time he did so, Aillen came, lulled everyone to sleep, and caused fires in the palace. This went on for over 20 years, all the way until Finn McCool joined the king's army and was invited to his grand Harvest Fest. Hearing about a creature even the bravest warriors of the Fianna were afraid of, Finn decided to form a plan to defeat Aillen. He knew he had to resist the creature's spell and stay awake. He placed his spear into a flame, heating it up. When it was glowing red, he pressed the tip of the spear to his head. The pain caused him to stay wide awake and alert, and when the goblin arrived, he plunged the spear into its body. The High King was so happy that the creature was no longer threatening his kingdom that he offered Finn any reward he desired. But Finn McCool only wanted one thing - and this was to become the leader of the Fianna. His wish was granted, and Cormac offered him full support in defeating Goll Mac Morna.

Despite his fame as a fearless warrior and being the High King's favorite, it's said that Finn became a just and fair leader, treating everyone serving under him equally. In fact, when his own son had a dispute with a stranger, he listened to both parties as if they were both strangers to him. When he determined that the quarrel was his son's fault, he ruled against him. According to another story, Finn even welcomed the son of one of his greatest enemies into his ranks. When the youngster decided to swear faith to him, he accepted it and trained him to become a fierce warrior. And while Aillen was no longer threatening Ireland around Samhain, Finn knew that they were always people in need on his land. So, after each harvest, he would gather food, drink, or anything else he could spare. He then ordered the goods to be given to people in need so they would have all the necessities during the harsh winter months. At the same time, Finn McCool was also said to be prideful and unforgiving towards those who hurt him or his closest ones.

Finn and Sadhbh

One day when Finn and his warriors were out hunting, his hounds Bran and Sceolan started to chase a deer. However, when they get close to the frightened animal, the hounds hunched down, protecting it instead of helping the warriors slay it. Knowing that the hounds themselves were once humans and were turned into an animal by magic, Finn suspected they felt the deer might be under a spell too. He took the deer home, where it turned into a beautiful woman. She said to him that her name was Sadhbh, and a dark Druid cursed her to live like a deer in the forest because she refused to marry him, but as soon as she set foot on the Fianna land, the curse was lifted.

Finn and Sadhbh fell in love, and they decided to marry and form a family. To keep her safe from the wrath of the dark Druid, he asked her never to leave the walls of his palace, and she agreed. However, one day, when Finn was forced to leave his beloved wife and the baby, she was expecting. Outsiders were invading Ireland, and his king asked Finn to defend the country. Thinking they would be safe inside the walls of his home, Finn left his family and went to battle the invaders.

Unfortunately, after only a week of Finn departing from Sadhbh, the Druid returned and tricked her into leaving the safety of the Fionna land. He came disguised as Finn, with two hounds resembling Bran and Sceolan, and asked Sadhbh to meet him outside the palace. Thinking Finn had a surprise for her or the child she was expecting, Sadhbh went ahead to greet him. But as soon as she stepped outside the palace, the Druid cast a spell, turning her into a deer once again.

Having defeated the enemy once again, Finn was very excited to return to his family - only to be greeted with the bad news that they were gone. Over the next few years, Finn went out on one quest after another, looking for Sadhbh, even taking his faithful hounds with him, hoping they would catch her scent, but it was in vain. Until one day, the hounds come across a fawn, whom they took into their protection, just as they did with Sadhbh. Finn realized that the fawn must be his son, and he took him back to his palace. Here it changed into a boy who said Sadhbh raised him in her deer form.

He also explained that the dark Druid had the two animals (the ones disguised as Bran and Sceolan) guarding them, fearing they would escape and return to Finn. When he visited, the Druid would bring them food and talk to Sadhbh, and every time she rejected him, he would grow angrier and angrier. One day he decided to separate Sadhbh from her son with another spell. The Druid pointed a hazel wand towards the deer, enchanting her to follow him, and then he touched the fawn and sent him to the clearing where his father's hounds found him.

Since he couldn't find Sadhbh, Finn decided to dedicate his life to raising his son, who he named Oisín, which means "little fawn." Having been raised in the wilderness, Oisín knew nothing about living in a home or being a warrior, so his father had his work cut out for him. Fortunately, under Finn's guidance, Oisín grew up to be a mighty warrior, making Finn and the Fianna proud. Apart from having his own adventures, Oisín also helped spread the tales about his father by becoming a poet.

The Pursuit of Diarmuid and Gráinne

When his son Oisin grew up, and Finn once again found himself alone, he decided to find a wife with whom he could share his days. The High King Cormac mac Airt promised him the hand of his daughter, Gráinne, a young and beautiful young woman. While hesitant at first, after noticing that she was also very wise, Finn agreed to marry her. However, Gráinne was already in love with a young warrior named Diarmuid - who was also Finn's friend.

Diarmuid and Gráinne met when they were younger and were separated by her father, who wanted her to marry a man with a better position. When her father told Gráinne that she must marry Finn McCool, she decided to put her dreams aside and obey. But it all changed when she saw Diarmuid again just before she got married. Seeing her at the wedding feast, Diarmuid tried to remember his duty to his chief, but he couldn't hide his love for Gráinne either. So, the two of them decided to run away and live hiding from Finn. Some legends say they moved from one place to another every few months, while others claim they slept at a different place every night.

Feeling hurt and betrayed, Finn began to chase them through Ireland, along with Oisin and the rest of the Fianna. He was very close to finding them a few times, but they always managed to elude him. Once, he came across a giant who had just been slain by a warrior. Knowing only the men trained by him were capable of such a skilled deed, he suspected that it was Diarmuid who did the slaying. It had only happened recently, and, at the time, all the other warriors were with Finn. In fact, it was so recent that he suspected that Diarmuid didn't even have time to get too far when the Fionna got there. He was right - Diarmuid was hiding in a tree just above his head. Fortunately for him, Finn and the Fionna were called away by duty as they went on to defend their king's land once again.

Finally, after many years of hiding with their growing family, Diarmuid and Gráinne decided to make peace with Finn. Seeing his former friend happy with his wife and children, Finn agreed to put his hurt aside, ending the pursuit. He let Diarmuid back into his ranks, and they became friends again. Together, they went out on many hunting trips, including the final one, in which a wild boar attacked Diarmuid. Desperate to save his life, Finn tried to get him to drink water from his hands. But by the time he got his friend, the water trickled through his fingers, and he couldn't save him. Diarmuid has moved on to the land of spirits.

Chapter 5

The Beautiful-but-Horribly -Unlucky Deirdre

The Ulster cycle mentions one King more than any others, King Conchubar Mac Neasa, and Deirdre's tragic tale starts with King Conchubar Mac Neasa's early kingship. The King was supposedly very young when he took over the kingdom from his foster father, Fergus Mac Roich. Although this agreement was supposed to last only for a year, the King showed such great promise that the people of his kingdom decided to let him stay King at the end of that year. During the early years of his Kingship, Conchubar and his court, including the warriors of the Red Branch, were invited over to a feast at Felimid mac Daill's house; he was the royal storyteller and harper of Emain Macha.

The feast was very extravagant as Felimid was very happy and excited about the upcoming birth of his firstborn child. The king's chief Druid, Cathbad, was a member of the king's court, and Felimid asked him to predict the baby's future. And so, Cathbad placed his hands near Felimid's wife's womb and started to work his magic. The Druid predicted that the baby would be a girl and not just any girl, but the most beautiful girl in the whole of Ireland. With time, the baby's beauty was to increase until she turned out to be extremely beautiful, so much so that many men would fight over her. As this sounded like a good fate, Felimid got very pleased hearing this. However, Cathbad continued to say, *"An excess of anything can be deadly, and the beauty of the girl will be a cause of great trouble between lords and kings."*

He went on to say that the daughter would tear the Red Branch apart and that Ulster's three greatest warriors would be sent into exile for her sake. When the men of the Red Branch heard this, they asked that the baby be slain right then and there so that she would never uphold the prophecy. However, King Conchobar, trying to be a wise and merciful king, forbade his warriors from doing so. He declared that he could not and would not allow the murder of a child in her father's home. Instead, he proposed that he send the child away to be raised in secret and that if she grew up to be as lovely as Cathbad had predicted, he would marry her himself so that no other man would dare to gaze at her. Not being able to say no to the King, Deirdre's father agreed.

For this purpose, the King's old nurse Leabharcham was assigned to keep the child with her hidden in a secret valley, away from any living human. The nurse was a kind woman, one tutored in finest talents that any courteous woman would require, and she grew to love Deirdre like her own. She taught Deirdre all the qualities and talents that a lady of royalty should have to make sure she made a fitting bride for King Conchobar. The King made sure to visit Deirdre from time to time to check on how she was faring, and as predicted by the Druid, she was growing up to be very beautiful indeed. And although the King was fairly good-looking and adored by his court, Deirdre showed no interest in him from the very beginning.

From the beginning, Leabharcham was very secretive about Deirdre because of the King's orders and never let her wander around outside of the hidden valley. In fact, there was no other person Deirdre came in contact with during her early years except for an old man who used to help the nurse with work. Leabharcham allowed him to visit the valley because he was mute and couldn't reveal Deirdre's secret to anyone else. During the onset of early springtime, with the snow still wet on the ground, the old man slaughtered a calf to make some food for Deirdre and Leabharcham, and the blood spilled onto the snow. During this, a raven came down to eat the calf's meat, and Deirdre seeing this, gave a sudden cry and fainted.

The nurse assumed that Deirdre must have gotten upset at the sight of all that blood, but when Dierdre got her consciousness back, she told the nurse that she had fallen in love with those three colors and would only love a man with these three colors. According to Deirdre's vision, she was supposed to love a man with snow-white skin, raven black hair, and blood-red cheeks. Leabharcham told Deirdre that there was, in fact, a man with these exact features. Upon asking, Leabharcham told Deirdre about the youngest son of Uisneach, Naoise, who was one of the best warriors in the Red Branch.

Naoise was regarded as the Red Branch's most attractive warrior, both brave and lovely. Ardan and Ainnle, his two brothers, were very attached to him. Deirdre knew she had to see him as soon as she heard about him. And so, Deirdre pressed Leabharcham to allow her to go see Naoise. Knowing Deirdre was intended to be the King's wife, Leabharcham rebuffed her demands. However, Deirdre was adamant, and she kept pestering Leabharcham until she ultimately caved in and consented to help Deirdre see Naoise.

Leabharcham planned an elaborate scheme to get Naoise to come to the hidden valley. When she went to Emain Macha, she enticed the sons of Uisneach to the secret valley she lived in by making them believe that it was an impressive hunting area. She also told Deirdre that she was only allowed to look at Naoise from afar, and under no circumstances should she come out of her hiding place. However, when the three brothers went to the hidden valley for hunting, Deirdre fell in love with Naoise at first glance, and she knew she had to meet him. So, she took Leabharcham's instructions and went out to meet Naoise. Naoise couldn't help but be captivated by Deirdre's beauty and charisma. Deirdre urged Naoise to run away with her because they were both in love, but he refused because Deirdre was intended to be the King's future bride.

Deirdre, smitten by Naoise, cast a geasa, or enchantment, on him, compelling him to flee with her. When he realized he didn't have a choice, Naoise set out to bring Deirdre as far away from Emain Macha as he could before the King found out. Ardan and Ainnle, Naoise's brothers, unwilling to be parted from him, decided to accompany the couple away from the kingdom, so the four of them, along with their slaves and retainers, escaped the land. Since there was no place in Ulster safe for Deirdre and Naoise anymore, the sons of Uisneach and Deirdre moved across the sea to Scotland.

In Scotland, Deirdre and Naoise made a home in the wilderness where she took care of him and his brothers, prepared fine meals for them, and took care of their every need. The brothers joined the King of Scotland's military and became members of his service. However, they chose not to stay in the fort with the other soldiers and left at the end of each day. Many of their comrades grew apprehensive and reported it to Scotland's King. He dispatched scouts to trail the three brothers into the wilderness and report back on what they were keeping concealed. The three brothers returned to a camp in the middle of nowhere, where they were welcomed by the most beautiful woman the soldiers had ever seen.

When the King of Scotland heard about this exquisite woman, he felt envious and wanted her all to himself. He couldn't kill his sworn soldiers, so he had to come up with alternative ways to be rid of them. Instead of murdering them outright, the King had them stationed at the front lines of battle. However, the brothers were such skilled warriors that they miraculously survived each fight. Deirdre became suspicious of the King's motives and encouraged Naoise to flee the dangers they were facing. So, they fled further into the wilderness and found a habitable island to make camp on. This is where they remained for a while.

King Conchobar's rage and resentment grew more by the day on the other side of the ocean in Emain Macha, but he couldn't do anything about Naoise and Deirdre because they were in another kingdom. Fergus Mac Roigh, one of the King's bravest and noblest warriors, was the only one bold enough to bring up the matter of the Sons of Uisneach. The King was furious at Naoise's betrayal; nevertheless, Fergus adored the sons of Uisneach and sought to persuade King Conchubar to spare them. Fergus persuaded King Conchubar to give in after a series of arguments and pleadings. or at least, such was Fergus Mac Roigh's belief. Fergus gladly accepted the King's request to bring the boys back to Ulster and put them under his protection.

In search of the sons of Uisneach, Fergus went to Scotland and let out a shout. At the exact time, far away in the wilderness, Deirdre and Naoise were playing chess. Hearing the shout, Naoise jumped up and said, "That sounds like the shout of an Irishman," to which Deirdre replied that it was the shout of a regular Scottish man. Fergus let out another shout, and this time Naoise was sure that it was the shout of a Ulsterman and that of his close friend Fergus Mac Roich, and this time, there was nothing Deirdre could do to make him believe otherwise.

When Naoise inquired why Deirdre had misled about Fergus's shout, she said she had witnessed a dream in which a raven flew from Ireland to Scotland with honey in its beak, but when it landed, the honey changed to blood. Fergus's presence in Scotland, Deirdre felt certain, was linked to the dream somehow. She was certain that whatever prospect he presented would not be fruitful for them.

However, the sons of Uisneach ignored her warnings, dismissing them as the work of a woman's vivid imagination.

Fergus informed them that the King of Ulster had pardoned Naoise and Diadre and wished them to return to their homeland. The brothers were overjoyed to learn this, as they had kept missing their friends and comrades. On the other hand, Deirdre was wary of the situation, believing it to be too good to be true. Deirdre never turned her gaze away from the Scottish coast on the voyage back to Ulster, singing laments about having to leave the wonderful land that had provided them all so much joy and peace.

As soon as they arrived on the shores of Ulster, the King arranged a local man to summon Fergus to a feast. . All the warriors of the Red Branch were under a geasa to never deny a meal in their honor. Fergus had little choice but to leave for the feast, secretly arranged at the King's behest by a local man. Deirdre had a keen sense of what was wrong and could detect when something wasn't quite right. She pleaded with Fergus not to abandon them, as she was certain something awful would ensue. However, Fergus could not deny the geasa and was forced to leave. Deirdre chastised him for abandoning the people he was supposed to protect. To satisfy her, Fergus left his son, Fiachu, with Deirdre and the brothers to ensure they were protected.

The King personally did not come out to greet the group when they arrived at Emain Macha, instead of sending Leabharcham. They were taken to the Speckled House, which served as a safe haven for Red Branch soldiers; Deirdre was urged to conceal her face to avoid unwanted attention. Deirdre and Naoise played chess to pass the time while Leabharcham served them food and drinks.

When the King asked about Deirdre from Leabharcham to appease the King, she replied that Dierdre had lost all her beauty in the wilderness and was now a withered old hag. However, Conchubar was untrusting of her word and sent another one of his spies to get a glance at how Deirdre fared.

The servant proceeded to the Speckled House and peered in the window. The fabric covering Deirdre's face had slid away, revealing her lovely face to the servant. When Naoise noticed the man staring at Deirdre through the window, he threw a chess piece at him, knocking out one of his eyes. When the servant returned to the King, he said Deirdre looked as beautiful as ever and that he'd willingly have his other eye removed if it meant he might see the beautiful Dierdre once more.

When the King learned of Dierdre's retained beauty, he felt betrayed once more. His burning jealously and rage resurfaced, and this time Deirdre and Naoise found themselves in his Kingdom, under his rule. The King ordered his troops to attack Uisneach's sons, but half of his men hesitated to slaughter their former comrades in arms. The other half prepared to attack the Speckled House.

Uisneach's sons prepared to fight the incoming army and put Deidre in their midst; then, they stood shoulder to shoulder in a circle around her. They vowed to protect Deidre at any cost. No matter how many men came at them, they could bravely fend them off. Although they were fewer in number, they used to be a part of the Red Branch and were still among the fiercest warriors of Ulster.

Fergus Mac Roigh's son, Fiachu, fought in the attack alongside the three brothers honoring his pledge to his father to protect the sons of Uisneach under any circumstances. He came face to face with King Conchobar's son in combat. Conall Cearnach of the Red Branch saw someone attacking the King's son and struck down the offender without hesitation. However, when he saw that it was Fiachu he had killed, he struck the King's son as well.

The fighting carried on for a long time before King Conchubar realized that his troops were making little progress against the defensive party. He sought advice from Cathbad, the royal Druid, to find a better alternative. However, Cathbad would only help Conchubar if he pledged not to harm Uisneach's sons. The King consented, declaring that all he wanted was for Naoise to apologize and the feud to be over. So, the Druid conjured up a spell that engulfed the sons of Uisneach in an endless, deep, and hungry sea. This exacerbated the hardship of their struggle tenfold.

Uisneach's sons displayed remarkable bravery throughout it all and refused to give up. Naoise slung Deirdre over his shoulder and began swimming while fending off the assailants. However, all three of them were forced to give up due to exhaustion after a while. Seeing this as a good opportunity, Conchobar's men seized the three brothers and brought them to the King.

Because of his pledge to Cathbad, King Conchubar could not kill the brothers himself; instead, he vowed to reward any man who would do so for him with a fortune. However, none of the Red Branch's men were willing to carry out such a murder because Uisneach's boys were akin to their own. Finally, one man volunteered to carry out the task. He was the son of King Maigne Rough Hand of Norway, and he held a particular grudge towards Naoise for killing Maigne's father and siblings in a fight.

When it came time to execute the brothers, Ainnle requested to be executed first since he couldn't stand living without his brothers. He was the youngest and had never been separated from his brothers before, and he didn't want it to change now. Ardan, like Ainnle, wished to be slain first so he wouldn't have to watch his brother's death. Then Naoise came up with a plan to kill them all at the same time, eliminating the need for them to be separated. He presented Maigne his sword, which had been given to him by Manannan Mac Lir and could cut through anything in front of it. He requested that Maigne cut all of their heads off at the same time. Maigne obliged and cut off the heads of the sons of Uisneach in one swing of the sword.

Deirdre witnessed the execution but was powerless to stop her one true love from being murdered in cold blood. When the noble warrior Fergus returned from his feast and discovered the sons of Uisneach with their heads chopped off and his own son dead nearby, he felt betrayed and enraged, and he sought to set fire to Emain Macha. Then he and a few Red Branch fighters who had refused to participate in the massacre of innocents left Ulster. To atone, they went to Queen Maeve of Connaught, King Conchubar Mac Neasa's fiercest opponent, and vowed their allegiance to her.

After the battle, King Conchubar took Deirdre to court and made her his bride. He gifted her a beautiful horse, surrounded her with the finest luxuries, and provided anything a woman could dream of. However, Deirdre's hatred towards the King never cooled. She ignored every gift he presented her, no matter how grand, and took no interest in the luxuries he provided. After a year passed with this behavior, Conchubar ultimately grew tired of Deirdre's coldness.

After her death, Deirdre was buried in Emain Macha, close to where her husband Naoise and his brothers lay. However, king Conchubar was jealous of their love even after they were dead and hated the thought of them being close to each other. So, he had stakes of wood driven into the ground between where their bodies were buried. But even the wooden stakes couldn't keep the lovers apart, and two beautiful trees grew from their graves that twined together. In the end, Deirdre's prophecy was, in fact, fulfilled, with Ulster's three greatest warriors being exiled and dead. The King's Red Branch was split into half and ruined for her sake, and the tale ended tragically.

Chapter 6

The Cattle Raid of Cooley

When it comes to mythological tales from Ireland, there are enough to make up four full myth cycles and then some. However, as in all mythologies, some are grander and better known than others – and in Celtic mythology, there are none that are as grand or as well-known as the story of the Cattle Raid of Cooley.

You may have heard of another famous mythological story, the story of the Trojan War. That story comes from Greek mythology, and big parts of the story are told in one of the most famous books in literature, The Iliad. The Cattle Raid of Cooley story is so important in Celtic mythology that it is often known as "The Irish Iliad."

Background to the Cattle Raid

There are a few things you must understand first before you hear the story of the cattle raid.

The first is why cattle were so important in early Ireland. Like many other places in the world, in early Ireland, having cattle was a way to indicate a person's wealth – and the more cattle you had, the wealthier you were.

Added to this, some bulls were more desirable than others. If a bull was particularly good-looking or got many cows pregnant, all the wealthiest people in Ireland wanted him – including royalty. In fact, cattle were so important to the early Irish royals that stealing prized bulls from a rival's herd was often seen as a way of challenging them to a battle or showing their own importance. When the person who was stolen from appeared to take back their bulls, they would usually steal a bull from the thief in return.

Another thing to know is that Ireland was once divided into four parts or provinces. These were known as Ulster, Leinster, Connacht, and Muster, and each of them had its own royal family.

The story of the Cattle Raid of Cooley mainly concerns the royals of Ulster and Connacht.

The Two Bulls

The "cattle" that make up the "cattle raid" portion of the story are the two bulls, Finnbhennach and Donn Cuailnge.

The two bulls were once sidhe. Donn Cuailnge was Bodb Derg's (king of the Tuatha Dé Danann) pig-keeper, and Finnbhennach was the pig keeper Ochall Ochne, another king of the sidhe. However, the two fought and, during their quarrel, transformed into a series of animals. Finally, they became worms and were swallowed by two cows.

Those cows gave birth to two bulls, Finnbhennach and Donn Cuailnge. They were extremely fertile and were two of the most desired bulls in Ireland.

Donn Cuailnge was born into the herd of Dáire mac Fiachna, a cattle-lord from Ulster, and Finnbhennach was born into the herd of Medb, the queen of Connacht. However, Finnbhennach believed being owned by a woman was beneath him and instead moved to the herd of Ailill, Medb's husband and king of Connacht.

Medb discovered that because he owned Finnbhennach, her husband was now wealthier than her. She wanted to make them equal and decided she had to own Donn Cuailnge.

As a result, she sent a messenger to Dáire mac Fiachna, asking him to loan her Donn Cuailnge for one year. In return, she offered an enormous amount of treasure and money and even offered him the chance to be her lover. Because of her generous offer, Dáire agreed.

The problem started when Medb's messenger got drunk. As a result, he mistakenly told Dáire the truth – that if he hadn't agreed to lend Medb the bull, she would have stolen him instead. Dáire was so angry that he decided to back out of the deal – and that was the start of the Cattle Raid of Cooley.

The Raid Begins

Before the exchange with Dáire, Medb and Ailill had already gathered their army in their capital, Cruachan, but no one knew

73

why. With an army already ready, Medb decided that she would ride with them to Ulster and steal Donn Cuailnge for herself.

Among Medb's army are Ailill, her husband, and several men from Ulster, led by Fergus mac Róich.

Fergus's Story

Fergus is in Connacht because he has chosen exile from Ulster, his homeland.

The king of Ulster was a man named Conchobar. Deidre, the daughter of Conchobar's chief storyteller, was an extremely beautiful woman, and Conchobar wanted to marry her. However, she was in love with Naoise, a young warrior, and eloped with him and his two brothers.

After some time, Conchobar announces he has forgiven the two of them and sends his best warriors - Fergus, Fergus's son Fiachu, his own son Cormac, and Dubthach Dóeltenga – to help them return to Ulster safely. Due to a series of betrayals, Naoise, his two brothers, and Fiachu are murdered by the men of Ulster, and Conchobar forcibly marries Deidre.

As a result of these betrayals, Fergus, Cormac, and Dubthach decide to change their loyalties to Medb, and 3000 of their men follow them to Connacht. Additionally, Fergus also becomes a lover of Medb. As a result, Fergus and his men fight for Connacht during the cattle raid instead of fighting for Ulster.

Before she leaves, Fedelm, a prophetess, warns Medb that thousands of her men will die at the hands of Cú Chulainn. However, Medb would not listen and chose to ride out on the raid.

The Curse of the Ulstermen

Medb chooses this time for the raid because the men of Ulster are under a curse that prevents them from fighting for five days. Instead, they are forced to lie in bed, suffering from a mystical illness that worsens when they try to fight.

The source of this illness is the goddess, Macha. One of the three sisters who are thought to make up the triple goddess Morrigna (or Morrigan), she is the goddess of kingship, land, horses, and fertility.

According to legend, her mortal husband boasts during a chariot race organized by the king of Ulster that she can run faster than the king's horses. The king threatens to kill her husband unless he can prove his claim. Macha, though heavily pregnant, is forced to race the king's horses due to this.

The goddess wins the race but is in severe pain and gives birth to twins as soon as the race ends. Humiliated, she curses the king and all the men of Ulster – she says that when they are in "greatest need," they will find themselves "as weak as a woman in childbirth."

Worse, the curse would not just be suffered by the king and his men – rather, it would linger until nine generations of Ulstermen had suffered under it. Thus, this curse was known as ces noínden, "the debility of nine," or the Noínden Ulad, "The debility of the Ulstermen."

Due to the curse, Medb and her army had a significant advantage and should have won easily – if it weren't for Cú Chulainn.

The Young Cú Chulainn

Cú Chulainn was a demigod, the son of the god Lugh and the mortal woman Deichtine, the sister of King Conchobar mac Nessa of Ulster.

At birth, Cú Chulainn was named Sétanta. As a young boy, he accidentally killed the hound of the smith Culann in self-defense. As compensation, he vows to raise a replacement hound for Culann – and guard the smith's house until the replacement hound can do so. As a result, he is given the name Cú Chulainn, or "Culann's Hound."

According to prophecy, Cú Chulainn is meant to live a short life – but one in which he will earn everlasting fame. He starts training at seven, and his skills are such that he is sent to Alba Scotland) to be trained properly. After finishing his training, he marries Emer, daughter of Forgall Monach.

At the time the Cattle Raid of Cooley took place, Cú Chulainn was 17 years old and had returned from his training. As a teenager and a son of Lugh, he is not one of the Ulstermen – and so, along with the women and children of Ulster, he is spared from Macha's curse.

So, when Medb rides to Ulster, Cú Chulainn is the only one standing between her and the successful theft of the bull Donn Cuailnge.

The Cattle Raid Takes Place

As the only man of fighting age in Ulster, Cú Chulainn is forced to find a way to defeat Medb's army. He manages to kill hundreds of Medb's men each day, attacking them from afar with his deadly slingshot. Terrified of the bloodshed, Medb tries to bribe him – and when that fails, Fergus brokers an agreement between the two sides.

To stop the slaughter of Medb's men by Cú Chulainn, Fergus allows him to invoke his right of single combat, that is, his right to fight each man in Medb's army one-on-one. In exchange for their willingness to fight Cú Chulainn, Medb promises each of her champions glory or, later, the hand of her daughter, Finnabair.

As the story continues, Medb sends champion after champion from her army – and Cú Chulainn defeats all of them. The battles last for months, and Cú Chulainn's victory seems inevitable (it is not explained why the Ulstermen, whose curse should have lasted five days, are still ill).

The men who die at the hands of Cú Chulainn include:

- Fráech, son of the goddess Bébinn and husband of Finnabair. His body is carried off by a group of sidhe women, all wearing green.

- Etarcomol, Medb and Ailill's foster-son

- Nathcrantail, a "huge warrior" of Connacht

- Redg, one of Medb's bards, or satirists

The only man to fight Cú Chulainn and live is Láréne, though he is disabled for the rest of his life as a result.

Additionally, Medb occasionally breaks the agreement of single handed-combat and sends several men to try to ambush Cú Chulainn. However, the demigod is victorious every time.

During his battles, Cú Chulainn is visited by multiple members of the Tuatha Dé Danann. In one incident, he is visited by a beautiful young woman who claims to be the daughter of a king. She tells him she is in love with him, but Cú Chulainn refuses her.

Angry, she reveals that she is actually one of the aspects of the Morrigan – specifically, that of the goddess of war. In her anger, she interferes in his next fight against Lóch mac Mofemis. To do this, she transforms herself into various animals:

- She becomes an eel, who trips him in the shallow area of the river (ford) where he is fighting

- She turns into a wolf and causes cattle to stampede across the area

- She becomes a heifer (cow), who leads this stampede

However, as she changes forms, Cú Chulainn wounds her every time and manages to win his battle. When the battle is over, she takes the form of an old woman milking a cow with wounds similar to the ones that Cú Chulainn had given her while she was in her animal form.

She offers his three sips of milk from the cow, and with each sip, he blesses her, healing each of her injuries in turn. He also tells her that he would not have turned down her romantic interest in him if he had known she was the Morrigan.

After one battle where he is significantly injured, Cú Chulainn is also visited by Lugh, his father. It is during this meeting that he is told who his father is. Because of his injuries, Lugh puts him into a magical healing sleep for three days.

When Cú Chulainn wakes, Lugh has healed all his injuries. However, while he sleeps, the young warriors of Ulster, too young to be affected by the curse, decide to attack Medb and her army. This group was made up of 150 youths and was led by Follomain, son of King Conchobar.

Their attacks succeeded in killing 450 of Medb's men, but all 151 were also killed in the process.

When Cú Chulainn wakes up, he is told what happened, and it causes him so much distress that he goes into the ríastrad, or battle frenzy state. He attacks the Connacht camp and avenges the young boy six times over (that is, he kills 900 men of Medb's army).

After this, the series of one-on-one battles continue until Medb finally sends Fergus to fight Cú Chulainn.

Fergus, Ferdiad, and Cú Chulainn

Aside from being the father of Fiachu, Fergus was also the foster father of Cú Chulainn. Fergus was finally chosen to battle his foster son as the one-on-one battles progressed.

Neither party was willing to fight the other, and so Cú Chulainn agreed to lay down his arms and yield the fight if Fergus vowed to yield the next time they met in battle. Though Fergus returned alive, Cú Chulainn continued to kill Medb's men until she finally convinced Ferdiad to fight him.

Ferdiad was Cú Chulainn's best friend and foster brother, and the two of them had trained in Scotland under the same warrior woman. Given their history, the two are just about equal on the battlefield, with the only distinguishing features being Ferdiad's horn skin, which cannot be pierced by any weapon, and Cú Chulainn's barbed spear Gáe Bulg, which only the demigod can wield.

Medb goads Ferdiad into fighting his foster-brother, with poets ready to name him a coward if he does not fight. At the same time, she promises to become his lover and marry him to her daughter Finnabair if he fights and wins.

Cú Chulainn, unwilling to fight and kill his foster brother, begs Ferdiad to withdraw. However, Ferdiad will not do so, and after a grueling three-day fight, Cú Chulainn is victorious. However, he is too wounded to continue fighting and is carried away by healers.

The Ulstermen Arrive

Though Cú Chulainn cannot continue, he has bought Ulster enough time – the cursed Ulstermen are once again able to fight. King Conchobar mac Nessa vows that all the cows that have been stolen and women kidnapped during the ride of Medb and her army will be returned to their rightful homes.

Cú Chulainn sits on the sidelines, wounded. While he recovers, Fergus fights Conchobar and is ready to kill him before he is stopped by his foster son (and Conchobar's son), Cormac. Finally, Cú Chulainn recovers enough to enter the battle again – and, as he had agreed, Fergus yields to him, leaving the field and taking all his surviving men with him.

The loss of Fergus and the exiled Ulstermen causes panic among Medb's army. Her allies panic, forcing her to retreat. However, Cú Chulainn manages to catch up to her – but she begs him to let her live, and he does, even guarding her retreat so that none of the other Ulstermen can kill her.

The Two Bulls, Again

Though the cattle raid resulted in disastrous losses for her army, Medb is successful in that she is able to capture the bull Donn Cuailnge and bring him with her to Connacht.

When she reaches her castle, she and her husband pit Finnbhennach and Donn Cuailnge against each other, making them fight to see which of the bulls is stronger. Finally, Donn Cuailnge is successful and manages to kill Finnbhennach. However, in the process, he is mortally wounded.

The wounded bull wanders around Ireland with the body of Finnbhennach on his horns. As he wanders, he drops off pieces of the defeated bull. Wherever a piece of Finnbhennach's body was deposited, that place was given a name corresponding to that piece.

Finally, Donn Cuailnge manages to find his way back to his original home. There, the wounded bull finally dies of exhaustion, ending the tale of the Cattle Raid of Cooley.

After the Cattle Raid

The heroes that survived the Cattle Raid played other important roles in Celtic mythology. These include:

- Conchobar takes place in one last great battle, the Battle of Ros na Ríg. Sometime after the battle, he is killed as a result of a wound inflicted by the warrior Cet mac Mágach.

- Cormac is invited to take his father's place as king. However, he encounters a Connacht war party raiding Ulster. He defeats them, and, as a result, Medb sends her army after him, resulting in his death.

- Fergus stays in exile for 14 years in total. He is killed by a trick played on him by Ailill, who is jealous of his wife's love for him.

- Ailill is killed by the hero Conall Cernach on the orders of Medb, who catches him cheating on her.

- Medb is killed by Furbaide, the son of Eithne. Before her marriage to Ailill, she had been married to Connacht, but after having a son with him, she chose to leave him. After this, her father gave Connacht the hands of another of his daughters (and Medb's sister) Eithne in marriage. When Eithne was pregnant, Medb murdered her – however, Furbaide managed to survive long enough to be born. He grows up to kill Medb to take revenge for the murder of his mother.

- Cú Chulainn plays a significant role in many stories from Celtic myth, including the story of Bricriu's Feast and the death of Cú Roí. He is finally killed in battle with the sons of several of the men that he had killed during his adventures.

The Cattle Raid of Cooley is perhaps the most important work of Celtic mythology. Aside from influencing numerous works of Irish literature, it is also considered the country's national epic. It also influenced numerous other parts of Irish culture, including music.

Chapter 7

Tir Na N-Óg

The Otherworld of the Irish Celts was not believed to be in an unknown, inaccessible, and far-away place. Instead, the ancient Irish believed that this world was right here on Earth. The thing about Tir Na N-Og, or the Celtic Irish Otherworld, is that it's largely subjective. This means no solid features, descriptions, or characteristics are tied to this heavenly world. People, especially poets and writers, were free to visualize it and give it their own portrayals. While some offered a detailed insight into their perception of the Otherworld, others used vague and unclear hints to reference the Otherworld. The exact location of Tir Na N-Og is unknown, primarily because it differed so much in the minds of writers from one century to the other.

Often, Tir Na-N-Og was described as the typical fairy world. It was a realm that existed underground and could be accessed through hills, caverns, and mountains. According to this fairy lore, the Otherworld accommodated various races and classes of beings that were not visible to the naked eye, like deities, demons, fairies, and shades. Many writings described Tir Na N-Og as linked to the Sidhe folk, which refers to the underground palaces and dwellings that the fairies of Gaelic folklore occupied. This underworld was split into kingdoms and had numerous districts ruled under their own fairy kings and queens. As you recall, the Tuatha De Danann shrank themselves so they could live underground in their beloved lands of Ireland after they had been defeated in battle. They assumed ownership over the vast canals and places that lay beneath Ireland's landscape. Many regard them as the gods of harvest and agriculture. Society also tends to blame the fairies for troubles, like floods, famine, or drought that they can't really explain.

Old Irish manuscripts also often described the Tir Na N-Og to exist within the Western Ocean. They described the realm as if it were another version of the lost city of Atlantis. Not only that, but the Son of the Sea, Manannan Mac Lir, can also be considered the spin-off of an old Atlantean King. Manannan Mac Lir was among the divine kings of the fairy population. Being one of the Tuatha De Danann, his palace existed in the Otherworld rather than the physical lands of Ireland. The fairy kinks used horse-drawn chariots to travel between both worlds. His mystical horses galloped over the waves of the sea. Fairy women who wished to make the trip to the lands of Ireland were transported via magical, spirit-like boats. They were able to charm any mortal man they chose.

This chapter explores the Celtic Irish Otherworld. It provides a deep insight into the evolution of the Irish and covers some of the most prominent myths set in that place.

The Evolution of Tir Na N-Og

Irish manuscripts tell us that the Otherworld existed at all times. It is everywhere we go but is still invisible to many people. Writings suggested that you could enter Tir Na N-Og if you passed through a Sidhe or hollow hill, especially at certain times of the year like Beltane and Samhain. Many records suggest that all hollow hills were open at that time and that the mystical barrier that splits both worlds is weakened.

The concept of time is said to be quite different from the Otherworld to the physical world. According to some myths, the real world and the Otherworld are at opposite periods of the yearly cycle. In other lore, however, spending a few hours in the Otherworld would be the equivalent of at least a century in the real world. The Otherworld can also be entered via lakes, moats, and other bodies of water. Many tales refer to flooded cities and kingdoms, suggesting that they represent Tir Na N-Og.

Both modern and ancient references to the Otherworld commonly feature mentions of music. Many thought that hearing sad and mournful music and songs that allude to magic can signify that the Otherworld surrounds you. According to legend, Fin Mac Cumhaill meets a supernatural being who comes from Tir Na N-Og through a hollow hill located near Tara every nine years. Cumhaill then burns the royal place to the ground and plays a mystical instrument that makes people fall asleep. It is said that the magical harp of the Dagda can also cause people to fall asleep.

Abundance is also a common theme in modern and ancient sources on the Otherworld. It is one of the most recurrent themes in the tales. Irish legends and stories always incorporate this element in one way or another. Notice how you will read of a plethora of feasts, ornate trees heavy with fruit, and fields that are rich in crops and produce. If you look at it in the physical, human sense, you will find that these images and how they tie to the fertility of the Irish land are symbols of rightful and proper leadership. The way that a king acts and makes decisions is echoed in the universe and the general environment.

In Irish folklore, when the king is granted land, they are said to be ceremonially wedded to it. This personification honors the goddess of sovereignty, and is also a reflection of the significance of her actions as a ruler. If he shows himself, or Fír Flatheomon, or justice, the land would be very fertile and abundant. The population and the Tuatha would also be content and will continue to proliferate. However, if the king fails to lead righteously and rightfully, the land will lack crops, plagues will sweep the lands of Ireland, storms will be frequent, and the newborns will die or be deformed.

The modern perceptions of the Otherworld are mainly associated with the fairies. Many old traditions and beliefs, such as the concept of time discrepancies, altered reality, and the themes of abundance and music, still prevail. Instead of being able to enter the Otherworld through burial mounds, however, modern Celts explain that you can access the Tire Na N-Og through structures known as the "Fairy Forts." These monuments are profuse across the nation.

There are at least 30,000 "Fairy Forts," also commonly named lios or rath. These enclosed dwellings date all the way back to the middle ages. Even though they have been there for millennia, people are still wary of them. Because the majority of the population is afraid of dealing with these structures, many farmers give them a wide berth and plant around them in their fields even if they take up a fair amount of planting space. However, they're not to blame considering that Irish folklore is full of unpleasant stories about the outcome of those who try to tamper with the Fairy Forts.

There is nothing mystical about the way that the raths look. The monument is usually a piece of land encircled by trees. However, walking into these spaces may allow you to enter the Otherworld. There are many incidents regarding individuals who attempted to cut down fairy trees and encountered members of the Otherworld, who warned them about cutting into their doors. These spiritual beings will do anything to protect their dwellings and are quick to avenge them in case of harm. Some legends tell of people who have been subject to a great deal of destruction, and even death, after violating the Fairy forts.

Some people also reportedly found themselves in the Otherworld after falling asleep under a sacred tree or on the side of the road. There is a popular tale of a man who found himself in a majestic house after drifting off to sleep at the side of the road. This house is one of the swoon-worthy mansions of the Otherworld. They are filled with large tables groaning with a variety of foods, reflecting the abundance aspect of the Tir Na N-Og. However, it was believed that consuming any of the delicious and mouth-watering food would be a great mistake, as it would trap you in the Tir Na N-Og forever. For some reason, humans seem to receive this warning from a fellow family member, who normally happens to be a woman, who had been previously taken away by the fairies. These stories blur the lines between the ghost and fairy realms in the world of Irish folklore. The Land of Youth is usually depicted to be populated by dead humans along with the fairies or Tuatha.

One legend tells how Connla, the son of Cú Chulainn, could replenish his hunger by eating no more than just an apple that he found in the Otherworld. To his doom, however, he was forever trapped in the Otherworld. Another tale tells how the Norse goddess

Iðunn kept the other divine figures youthful by giving them her magical apples.

The Legend of Oisin and Niamh

Many moons ago, a young man named Oisin wondered about the vast lands of Ireland. He loved to explore the plateaus and moorlands with the other warrior-hunters of the time, known as the Fianna.

One day, when he was out hunting with them, he came across a sight for sore eyes. In front of his eyes was a gorgeous woman with long, flaming red hair. She rode a glistening, beautiful white mare. The sun shone brightly on the lady's hair, casting a mystical golden light all around her. The mare moved so smoothly and rhythmically that she looked as if she were floating over the surface of the land. Approaching the group of hunters, the maiden brought her mare to a stop. The horse thumped at the stones in the field stones with its hooves, sending out a small spark with each blow as it waited impatiently.

The woman, who introduced herself as Niah, the daughter of the kind of the Tir Na N-Og, had a voice that sounded like the gentle music that sounds like someone playing the harp. Oisin stepped forward to greet the alluring woman, immediately falling in love when his eyes met her gaze. Feeling the same way, Niamh offered to take Oisin with her back to Tir Na N-Og. He didn't hesitate much before swinging himself up behind her on the mare. Together, they galloped over the sea, right into Tir Na N-Og.

Oisin lived his whole life in Ireland, roaming its emerald, green pastures and overlooking the azure blue seas that bordered the land. He loved the nation deeply and believed that a more beautiful place could not possibly exist. The place was magical and exceptionally beautiful, and so he stayed to build a life together with Niamh. He joined his newly found love and the stunning white mare on adventures every day. Their love grew more and more profound with each passing moment, as Niamh was always happy to share the magnificence of her magical home with Oisin. Although three centuries went by, it only felt like one Earth day. In that realm, no one ever aged or felt sick. They were always joyful and youthful.

Despite the love he felt for Niamh and the outstanding beauty of the place, Oisin never felt entirely fulfilled. Some part of his soul was still lonely, which was strange, considering that no one in Tir Na N-Og experienced negative emotions like loneliness or the lack of fulfillment. Niamh tried to relate to Oisin to understand the way he felt. However, she could never make him feel better, so she couldn't fight him back when he told her that he wished to return to Ireland and reunite with his family and the Fianna once again.

Niamh let him take the white mare back to Ireland but warned him against letting his foot touch the lands of Ireland. He rode across the sea and back to his homeland with great anticipation. However, his excitement dissipated as soon as the horse's hooves landed on the land of Ireland. Glancing at his home, now covered in ivy, Oisin realized that all had changed and that his friends and family were no longer alive.

Grieving his loss, yet still trying to track down his family, Oisin had completely forgotten to care for the mare. However, the compliant horse still responded to his commands despite being tired and hungry. When he finally came to terms with the fact that he was looking for a needle in a haystack, Oisin decided to ride the mare back to Tir Na N-Og.

He moved toward the sea, where he met a group of men who worked in a field on his way. Too tired to carry on, the mare stumbled over a rock and fell. Oisin thought that taking a piece of Ireland back to the Otherworld with him would help make him feel better. He reached his hands out to pick up the stone but lost balance and fell right onto the ground. At that moment, Oisin immediately aged 300 years. The mare reared and galloped straight to the ocean so she could go back to Niamh and her homeland.

The men who worked in the field were stunned at the sight. Besides the young man who aged right in front of them, they also witnessed a tired horse turn into a beautiful silvering white mare that rushed into and over the sea. They went to pick him up and take him to St. Patrick. Upon his arrival, Oisin told the saint all about Niamh, Tir

Na N-Og, how he lived there for three centuries, his family, and the Fianna. By the end of his story, Oisin was weary and tired. He closed his eyes and rested peacefully for eternity.

King Cormac's Journey to Tir Na N-Óg

King Cormac mac Airt was paid a visit by a gray-haired warrior who carried a silver tree branch. The branch had three golden apples that played relaxing music. The warrior, who we will later come to know as Manannán mac Lir, was dressed in a golden shirt, a purple mantle with fringe, and bronze sandals. He said he came from a land where people don't age, scandals never happen, and negative emotions like hatred and sadness aren't experienced. Then, Cormac asks to form an alliance with Manannán. The visitor agrees to give him the branch in exchange for three favors. While he doesn't name them right away, we would come to find out that these favors are Cormac's wife, son, and daughter.

When his wife disappears, Cormac follows her kidnapper and magically finds himself in misty land that houses two fortresses. He enters one of them to find a bronze and silver palace and a fountain decorated by the Ulster goddess Buan's purple hazel trees. The nuts that come from the trees roll into the fountain for five salmon fish to feed on, and the inhabitants of the palace drink from the water of the fountain, which sounds incredibly melodious.

Cormac is then met by a couple as soon as he enters the place: a warrior and a blonde woman. At that moment, a cook carrying an ax, a log, and a pig, walks into the palace to prepare a meal in a cauldron. When Manannán asks the cook to turn the pig, they explain that the pig will not be prepared until four truths are told.

The cook starts by telling how he once stole cattle from a man and only agreed to return them in exchange for the ax, log, and pig he had. The cook has been trying to cook the pig ever since the incident occurred. The warrior recounted a time when his people wanted to plow, plant, and harvest wheat, and all these steps were magically completed. He says that his people have been eating from the harvest ever since the incident occurred. The woman says that the seven cows and seven sheep she owns are enough to sustain the entire population of the Land of Promise. When asked to speak of his truth, Cormac decides to tell the story of the silver branch up to the present moment. The four truths were told, the pig was finally cooked, and Cormac was served his portion of the food. He stated to them that he could only eat within the presence of fifty men.

The warrior puts Cormac to sleep by singing a song. He wakes up to find the 50 men he requested and his wife, son, and daughter. Manannán mac Lir then tells Cormac his true name and explains that he just wanted to bring him to the Otherworld. Manannán said he would be returning everything he took from Cormac (his wife, son, and daughter). However, he explained that when Cormac dies, his wife, son, and daughter will automatically return to Tir Na N-Og.

The Otherworld that lies in the middle of the ocean has numerous names, suggesting that it's The Land of Youth, the Living, and Promise. Other names also mean "The Great Plain" and "The Plain

Happy." It was widely believed that those who visit this land or inhabit it experience no pain. They are never subject to aging and its effects and are therefore immortal. The Otherworld lacks the negative aspects of the mortal plane. There, there are no scandals, crimes, or sins. People who live in the Otherworld were thought to enjoy a life abundant in feasting, happiness, and joy.

Chapter 8

The Children of Lir

W e've already covered some of the most important stories from Celtic mythology, including the adventures of Finn McCool and the story of the Cattle Raid of Cooley. However, there are still some stories left to tell – including one of the most well-known, the story of the Children of Lir.

Celtic Myth and Christianity

For centuries, people of the Celtic world believed that their Celtic mythology was real, as were the gods and goddesses mentioned in it. Celtic mythology survived mostly unchanged, even when the Romans ruled Celtic society, although the Romans did borrow some of the Celtic gods to worship.

However, by the 4th century AD, the Roman emperor had made a rule that all Roman lands were supposed to covert to – and worship – Christianity.

This rule affected the Celtic world as well. By the 5th century AD, Christianity was already affecting how people thought of Celtic mythology, and by the 7th century, the old Celtic mythology was more or less ignored.

However, the Christian church had to explain to the common people why they should choose Christianity over Celtic mythology. To explain this, they created legends for a real Christian saint, Saint Patrick.

According to legend, he came to Ireland in the 5th century. He is said to have performed many great feats, including chasing all the snakes from Ireland into the sea and speaking to two great heroes from Celtic myth, Caílte mac Rónáin, and Oisín. Due to his efforts, he is said to be the person who introduced Christianity to Ireland and is still held in high regard in Ireland today.

However, the legends of Saint Patrick do not stop with him introducing Christianity to the county. Many stories explain how many people who believed in Celtic gods and goddesses decided to become Christians instead, and most of them were written long after the 5th century. These stories combine both Celtic mythology and Christianity, two important religious traditions in Ireland – and one such story is that of the Children of Lir. This story was likely first written in the 14th century but has since become an important part of Celtic myth.

Lir and His Four Children

The story of the children of Lir centers on several members of the Tuatha Dé Danann, the supernatural race of people who play an important role in many Irish myths. At the time of the story, they were losing power in Ireland, while the Milesians, another group of people who had sailed to Ireland from Iberia (in today's Spain and Portugal), were becoming more powerful.

During this time, Bodb Derg, the son of the god the Dagda, was elected as the king of the Tuatha Dé Danann. However, this election upset the sea god Lir, who believed he would have been a better king.

Bodb Derg did not want a war between the members of the Tuatha Dé Danann, so he looked for ways to get Lir on his side. Around this time, Lir's wife died – and so, Bodb Derg offered the sea god the hand of one of his daughters, Aoibh, in marriage.

Lir agreed and, in return, gave up his claim to the throne, resulting in an alliance between the two.

The marriage between Lir and Aoibh was a happy one, and they had four children:

- Fionnghuala, their only daughter

- Aodh, their eldest son

- Fiachra and Conn, twin boys

However, after giving birth to the twins, Aoibh died, causing a lot of grief to Lir. Knowing his son-in-law had four children to look after on his own, Bodb Derg offered Lir the hand of another one of his daughters in marriage – Aoife.

Lir, who remembered his marriage with Aoibh, accepted the offer, and the two were married.

Aoife's Jealousy

Lir's four children were loved by both their father and grandfather. However, their new stepmother soon grew jealous of the love they were given, and she began plotting her revenge.

First, she pretended she was very ill. After a year, she took the children to a river, telling her followers to ride behind their chariot. Firstly, she tried to convince them to kill the children, saying that Lir no longer loved her because of them. She promised them rich rewards in exchange for their help, but none were willing to kill innocent children.

So, she attempted to do the deed herself, pulling out her sword – but she found she could not kill the children either.

By then, the chariot carrying Aoife and the four children had arrived on the shores of Loch (lake) Dairbhreach. There, she told them to take a refreshing bath in the lake's cool waters – but once the children were in the water, she used her magical powers as a member of the Tuatha Dé Danann to turn them into swans.

Fionnghuala, who knew a little of magic, told Aoife that she had caused her own doom in doing so. Aoife, she explained, was not powerful enough to undo her spell and turn the children human again – but neither would anyone else be able to break the spell. Instead, Aoife's only hope was that she could set a time limit to the spell, after which the children would return to their human form.

Aoife, however, was unwilling to listen to her stepdaughter's words. She set a period of 900 years before the spell would break – and said that the children would spend 300 of those years on the waters of Loch Dairbhreach, the next 300 on the Sruth na Maoilé (that is, the Sea of Moyne between Ireland and Scotland), and the final 300 at Iorrus Domnann and Inis Gluairé (Inis Glora). Additionally, the spell would only expire when Lairgenn, the great-grandson of the current King of Connacht, was married to Deoch, the great-granddaughter of the current King of Munster, ending the enmity between the two kingdoms.

However, she did feel some guilt – and so she allowed the children to keep the ability to speak like humans, saying that they would spend the 900 years as swans singing the saddest songs Ireland had ever known. Additionally, she swore that the children would not be bothered by being swans.

The First Three Hundred Years

Having cast her spell on the children, Aoife left for her father's court. However, Badb loved his grandchildren, and he asked his daughter why they had not come with her to visit him.

Aoife told her father that Lir did not trust her to travel with his children. However, Badb was suspicious and sent messengers to his son-in-law immediately.

When Lir received the messengers, he knew immediately that Aoife had caused some harm to his children. He quickly made his way to Badb's court and, on the way, stopped at Loch Dairbhreach.

In the form of swans, his children told him the story of their curse and Aoife's actions. Lir and people grieved, and Lir begged his children to live with him until the end of their curse – but Aoife's words meant that that was not possible. Instead, Lir'sfollowers stayed with their leader by the shores of Loch Dairbhreach for the night, listening to the swans sing.

In the morning, they set out once again to Badb's court, and when they reached it, Lir told his father-in-law of Aoife's cruel actions.

When he heard what had happened to the children, Badb was furious because he knew that he had lost his daughter Aoibh, but he would also never see his grandchildren in their human form again. He turned to Aoife in anger and told her that her spell had cursed her more than the children.

The children, Badb told Aoife, would one day return to their human form. Aoife, however, would suffer forever. He then demanded she tells him what creature she would be most horrified to be turned into.

Aoife, terrified of her father's wrath, said that she would most hate to be a demon of the air – that is, a bat. "So be it," said Badb, who was a powerful magic user in his own right and turned her into a demon of the air with a strike of his wand. The demon that had once been Aoife let out a shriek and flew away, and it is said that she will remain in the form of a demon of the air, the form she hated the most, until the end of days.

However, though Aoife had been punished for her cruel actions, the children were still swans. As they couldn't leave the waters of Loch Dairbhreach, Lir, Bodb, and the rest of the Tuatha Dé Danann would travel to the Loch to visit them and hear their songs.

The children's music was so beautiful that other people of Ireland visited, including the Milesians, and the songs helped them all enter a state of calmness. Though their songs were plaintive, their beauty was enough to make the sad happy and help people who were full of grief or suffering an illness to forget their sorrows for a while.

And so, the children sang on the waters of Loch Dairbhreach for 300 years. While there were wars and chaos in the rest of the country, their region remained peaceful. Kingdoms rose and fell over the years, and still, they sang – and so, the first three centuries came to an end.

The Second Three Hundred Years

When their time on the waters of Loch Dairbhreach ended, the children flew from the lake and made their way to the Sruth na Maoilé. The people who lived around the loch were grieved to see the children leave and, in honor of their time there, decreed that no swan would ever be killed within the country of Ireland.

Finally, the four swans reached their destination – however, during the 300 years they had spent on Loch Dairbhreach, the Sea of Moyle had changed, and it was no longer the peaceful and wooded place they had known when they were human. Instead, the sea was wild, and the shores were filled with craggy rocks and steep cliffs.

The storms were so rough that, for a period, the children were separated and spread across the sea. After years, they were finally reunited but could not leave the cold and cruel waters due to Aoife's words.

Finally, they were visited by a troop of warriors from the Tuatha Dé Danann, led by Aodh and Fergus, who were the sons of their grandfather Badb. The warriors were delighted at finding the children, whom they had been looking for since they left Loch

Dairbhreach, and told the children the good news of their father, grandfather, and the rest of the Tuatha Dé Danann.

But the warriors could not stay, and they could not take the children with them, so they returned to their kingdoms. But the remaining Tuatha Dé Danann were glad to know that the children lived and were content knowing this.

The Final Three Hundred Years

Finally, the second set of three hundred years passed, and it was time for them to leave the Sruth na Maoilé. So, the children flew away and made their way to Iorrus Domnann and Inis Gluairé.

There they found the waters they were to live in were colder than the waters of the Sea of Moyle, and the storms were stronger. So strong were the storms and so cold the winds that the children nearly froze, and their feet turned to ice.

Terrified, the four children cried out to the "King of Heaven," vowing the honesty of their belief in him and begging him to protect them. Their pleas were heard, and they were protected from the worst of the storms from then on.

The Tuatha Dé Danann could no longer visit the children at Iorrus Domnann, but the sailors and fishermen who traveled the waters would often hear them singing. Here, the children encountered a young man to whom they told their life story.

And so, the final three hundred years passed.

Nine Hundred Years Later

When the nine hundred years of their curse were concluded, the children wondered where they should fly to. They debated for a long time before deciding to go to Sioth Fionnachaidh, Lir's castle.

However, when they reached the castle, they found that it was no longer the strong fortress they had once known. Instead, it had crumbled and was overgrown with plants, and so they decided to make their way to Inis Gluairé, thinking they would spend the rest of their days in the place they had lived last – for they knew that the ruins at Sioth Fionnachaidh meant their father was lost to them in this life.

At Inis Gluairé, the birds flocked around them, and they lived in peace for a time. However, one day they heard the sound of bells ringing and saw a priest robed in white. This was Saint Patrick, and his arrival signified the coming of Christianity to Ireland.

With him came the monk Mochaomhóg, who made his way to Inis Gluairé. He rang the bells again, calling matins, and hearing the bells so close to them that the three boys and the other birds were scared.

Fionnghuala, however, knew better, saying that the sound of the bells meant that it was time for them to be free from the curse. Hearing their sister's words, the boys agreed to listen to the bells – and when they stopped ringing, the children sang one of their songs as beautifully as ever.

Hearing this song, Mochaomhóg set out to search for the singers and finally came upon the swans. Seeing that the swans had sung the song, he asked them if they were the Children of Lir – for he had read the work of the young man they had spoken to at Iorrus Domnann and Inis Gluairé and knew of them. He said that it was his search of themthat brought him to Inis Gluairé in the first place.

Hearing his words, the children decided to trust him and allowed him to bind them using silver chains. They spent some time in the company of Mochaomhóg, and with him, they felt neither tired nor distressed at their lot in life. Seeing them in the company of the monk, the people of Inis Gluairé spread the story of the swans far and wide.

The story eventually reached Deoch, the great-granddaughter of the king of Munster and (as Aoife had foretold) wife to Lairgnen, the great-grandson of the king of Connacht and the current king. Deoch desired to have the swans for herself and asked her husband to get hold of them and gift them to her.

Lairgnen, wanting to please his wife, sent messengers to Mochaomhóg, asking him to sell the Children of Lir. However, Mochaomhóg refused, which made the king furious. In his anger, he moved toward Mochaomhóg himself and attempted to take the swans from him by force.

However, as soon as he touched the swans, their feathers fell off, and in their place stood three old men and one old lady. As Aoife had foretold, the marriage between Lairgnen and Deoch played a crucial role in returning the children to their human forms.

In seeing the Children of Lir now human again, Lairgnen left, leaving them to the monk.

After 900 years as swans, the children – now elderly – were very thin and bony. When he saw them, Mochaomhóg knew that they were not long for this world, and Fionnghuala knew it too.

Recalling their promise to the "King of Heaven," Fionnghuala asked the monk to baptize them, and he did. Once baptized into Christianity, the children, who were very old, died – but in death, they had transformed into children once again, as they had been before their stepmother cursed them.

As Badb had foretold, the children were free from their suffering – but Aoife's suffering continued, and she lives on in her bat-form.

The Children of Lir Today

The story of the Children of Lir is a myth that represents the movement of Ireland and Irish society away from the Celtic gods and goddesses toward Christianity. Though members of the Tuatha Dé Danann, the Children of Lir recognize the authority of the Christian "King of Heaven" over their fellows, who have magical powers, indicating the worldview of the time – that Christianity was better than other, "pagan" religions.

However, this story has left its mark in many other ways as well. It has inspired several Irish artists' musical compositions, songs, and albums. And several statues in the country take inspiration from the story for their design. The story of the Children of Lir has also been written and retold by several authors over the years, including 21st-century authors.

Furthermore, some people suggest that it is one of the inspirations behind the famous Russian ballet Swan Lake. However, while there are similarities between the stories, there is no evidence to suggest that it was inspired by Celtic mythology or this story specifically. Rather, it drew inspiration from several Roman and German folk tales.

While there is no link between the story of the Children of Lir and Swan Lake, it is undeniable that the story continues to influence artists and other creators to this day. Though it was written much later than many of the "classic" Celtic myths, its importance in telling a story that bridges the gap between Celtic and Christian Ireland means that it is truly a mainstay and an integral element of Celtic mythology.

Chapter 9

The Inevitable Demise of Cu Chulainn

The Death of Cú Ruí

You're familiar with Cu Chulainn and his feats of heroism from the story of The Cattle Raid of Cooley, but Cu Chulainn's heroic life came to an end at a very young age. The events that led to his ultimate demise started with another one of his adventures.

On this adventure, he is accompanied by Cú Ruí mac Dáire, the King of Munster, and a sorcerer who can change form. Cú Ruí takes part in a raid of Inis Fer Falga, or the Isle of Man, led by the Ulaid and Cu Chulainn, but only on the condition that he would be given the choice of spoils from the raid. The group succeeds in stealing treasure and cattle and also abducting Blathnát, daughter of the island's King. During this, Blathnát fell in love with Cu Chulainn because of his strength and bravery, but Cú Ruí had also taken a fancy to Blathnát's beauty. So, Cú Ruí demanded Blathnát as his share of the spoils. When Cu Chulainn tried to stop Cú Ruí from taking Blathnát, Cú Ruí got the better of him. He cut off Cu Chulainn's hair and drove him to the ground up to his armpits before escaping with Blathnát.

Later, Cu Chulainn made a plan to meet Blathnát; he went through a long journey to meet her on Samhain, the first day of winter. This was when they came up with a plan to end Cú Ruí's life, as he could only be killed in contrived circumstances. Blathnát discovered this secret and told Cu Chulainn how the deed was to be done. Their plan was to kill Cú Ruí when he was unarmed and vulnerable. Blathnát was to pour milk down the stream when she was washing Cú Ruí so that the river's stream moving towards the Ulster army turned white. This was the signal that Cú Ruí was in his room unarmed, and they would be able to attack him and his stronghold. Cú Ruí did not hear a single thing until Cu Chulainn and his men were upon him. Cu Chulainn and the Ulstermen then killed Cú Ruí and took over his fort. However, before Cu Chulainn and Blathnát could be reunited, Ferchertne, Cú Roí's poet, in the act of rage, seized Blathnát and threw himself over a cliff, killing himself and Blathnát.

The Alliance of Queen Medb with Cu Roi's Son

Queen Medb was still angry about her defeat in The Cattle Raid in Cooley and wanted to exact revenge on Cu Chulainn. Luckily for her, there were a number of other people who also wanted revenge from the great warrior. Most of these enemies were wronged spouses or children whose parents had been murdered by Cu Chulainn. One of these enemies was Cú Ruí's son, Lugaid Mac Cu Roi, who wanted nothing more but to avenge his father by killing Cu Chulainn. Queen Medb saw this situation as a good opportunity to kill Ulster's greatest warrior and weaken the kingdom's army even more. And so, Queen Medb formed an alliance with Lugaid Mac Cu Roi and the offspring of Calatan, a great sorcerer Cu Chulainn had killed.

Cu Chulainn and the sorcerer had had a faceoff in one of the earlier wars between Ulster and Connacht during The Cattle Raid of Cooley (Táin Bó Cúailgne). This was when Cu Chulainn killed the powerful sorcerer, and this was the point where Cu Chulainn's fate was sealed. When Calatan died, his wife was pregnant with sextuplets, and after a while, she gave birth to six children; 3 girls and 3 boys. All of these children grew up to be as powerful as their father and were taught the expert druid magic that their father had. Since the moment they had consciousness, their mother had instilled within them hate so deep for the murderer of their father that the children had made it their life's purpose to get revenge for their father's murder.

Cu Chulainn, fully oblivious to all of these schemes, continued on with his life after the war for several years. When the timing was opportune, Calatan's offspring came together with Lugaid Mac Cu Roi and, with the support of Queen Medb, devised the ideal plot to finally put an end to Cu Chulainn's reign. When Conchubar Mac Neasa, King of Ulster, learned of the plot, he did all he could to safeguard Cu Chulainn. Cu Chulainn was one of the King's most powerful warriors, and without him, Emain Macha, and possibly all of Ulster, would be disrupted. To protect Cu Chulainn, he invited the warrior to come to stay with him in Emain Macha. The King tried to keep Cu Chulainn's attention with any kind of attractions he could muster up. There were various sports, feasts, and other revelries to keep Cu Chulainn distracted during this time. Conchubar knew if he let Cu Chulainn get even the wind of this threat, he'd go out to face it head-on.

But the plan for Cu Chulainn's demise was already underway, and nothing could stop it. Calatan's three daughters and sons traveled to Emain Macha and employed their Druid magic to create terrifying war sound all around the city. The clamor was deafening and impossible to ignore. People could hear weapons striking, battle screams, feet stomping, and the cries of people suffering all around the city. However, Conchubar was prepared for any kind of attack Cu Chulainn's enemies might try. To drown out the sounds of battle, he summoned all of his men to the palace for a large feast. The feast included such enthralling singing and storytelling and drinking and partying that the sounds from the fake war outside were drowned out.

This strategy succeeded for three days and nights, keeping Cu Chulainn engaged and oblivious to outside noises. But the magic seemed to last as long no matter how long, kept the feast going, and showed no indications of slowing down. Conchubar realized this and knew he needed to devise a new strategy to divert his nephew's attention away from the outside threat. Conchubar came up with a solution by summoning his entire court to Gleann na mBodhar, often known as the Valley of the Deaf. The valley's name comes from the notion that no outside noises, real or imagined, could enter the valley. This way, no matter what magical noises the children of Catalan brewed, they couldn't enter the valley, and Cu Chulainn would not be able to hear them.

Conchobar's plan worked successfully since he could keep the war voices at bay while keeping Cu Chulainn unharmed. The sorcerers quickly realized that no matter how loud their noises were, they wouldn't be able to penetrate the Valley of the Deaf. So, the daughters of Calatan devised a new scheme in which one of them pretended to be Niamh, one of Cu Chulainn's companions. She then entered the valley and requested Cu Chulainn's assistance in combat. Cu Chulainn, ever the valiant warrior, seized at the chance for a challenge and the chance to help a comrade in need.

Cu Chulainn gathered his weapons and retrieved his horse, Lia Macha, the Gray of Macha, to attach her to his chariot. However, for the first time since Cu Chulainn had tamed Lia Macha, she appeared to be frightened at the idea of fighting. He attempted to retrieve her a second time, but she moved away again as if she sensed terrible doom awaited them on the battlefield. Cu Chulainn chastised her on his third effort, and upon hearing this, the horse eventually agreed to be saddled, but she shed bloody tears as she imagined the loss that lay ahead. As Cu Chulainn awaited his mother's departure, he summoned his charioteer, Laeg, to take the reins of the chariot.

Cu Chulainn's mother, Deichtre, would always offer a cup of wine as a farewell before going into battle. She believed it was her wish for him to be safe throughout the conflict. When she handed him a cup of wine to bless him this time, however, the drink turned to blood as soon as he lifted it to his mouth. Deichtre was perplexed, so she summoned another cup of wine, which, once again, changed to blood as soon as Cu Chulainn drew it close to his mouth. After a third attempt, Cu Chulainn gave up on the wine and went to combat.

And so began Cu Chulainn's ultimate journey towards his death, a journey he did not know he was making. He observed an old woman cleaning his armor in the river as he was crossing a ford. "I'm polishing the armor of the great warrior who is going to die today," the old woman said to him as he walked by. Cu Chulainn, who was not terrified of superstitions or forewarnings, dismissed it and continued on his way.

After a bit, he came upon a group of 3 old crones on the roadside, cooking something. When he got close enough, he noticed they were cooking a hound on a spit. As the noble warrior he was, he came to a halt to meet them, and the old hags welcomed him to join their supper. Like every other warrior in the Red Branch, Cu Chulainn was bound by a geasa to never consume dog meat, so he graciously declined the offer. The hags persisted, mocking him, and implying that he was used to exquisite meals and would not eat this dinner with them.

Cu Chulainn was an honorable warrior through and through, and he was stuck in a conundrum. He could turn down their hospitality and prove them right about him being too proud and thinking he was superior, or he could ignore the geasa and share the meal with them. He went with the latter alternative and sat down to share the food with hags. He picked up the meal with his left hand, and as soon as it reached his lips, he lost all strength in that hand. The meat fell onto his thigh almost immediately, and as soon as it did, all of his thigh's strength ebbed away with it. He realized he had broken the geasa and had been punished as soon as he arose.

The hags then turned out to be Morrigan, the goddess of war. She had taken her revenge on him because Cu Chulainn had done something in the past and now regretted it. Long before, Morrigan had fallen in love with Cu Chulainn and offered him her love. However, Cu Chulainn, not knowing who Morrigan was, rejected her. Although Cu Chulainn was weakened because of the broken geasa now, he didn't let it stop his journey. He went on until he encountered the three sons of Calatan, one by one, in a scheme planned precisely to kill Cu Chulainn.

There had been a prophecy regarding Cú Chulainn's three spears that he would throw in the upcoming battle, wielding powerful magic. It was predicted that these spears would kill three kings, so Cú Chulainn's enemies were very interested in getting their hands on them. To do that, they set up different schemes.

Erc, son of Cairpre Nía Fer, is another one of Queen Medb's acquaintances whose father was killed by Cú Chulainn in Cath Ruis na Ríg, "The Battle of Ros na Ríg". He sends two of his men pretending to fight and a satirist to shame Cú Chulainn into breaking the fight. One of the sons of Calatan is disguised as the Satirist, who, after Cú Chulainn breaks the fight by killing the combatants, asks for his spear. He threatens to satirize Cú Chulainn for his stinginess unless he gives him his spear. So, to defend his generosity, Cú Chulainn throws his spear through the Satirist's head. This is when the son of Cu Rio, Lugaid, takes this spear and throws it toward Cú Chulainn. However, the spear misses and hits Laeg Mac Riangabra and kills him instantly. The sons of Calatan tell Lugaid that Laeg was the King of the Charioteers, and thus the spear, in fact, did kill a king.

Erc again sent two of his men to fight, which forced Cú Chulainn to break the fight apart by killing them. Again, Calatan's second son, disguised as a satirist, asks for Cú Chulainn's spear. But this time, Cú Chulainn refuses to give him the spear, saying that he had shown enough generosity. However, the Satirist threatens to curse the Ulaid this time, which forces Cú Chulainn to defend Ulster's honor. He threw the spear through the second son's head and said, "Never let it be known that Ulster fell because of its champion warrior." Lugaid Cu Roi again pulled the spear out of the body and threw it towards Cú Chulainn. However, the spear misses again and instead hits Cú Chulainn's loyal horse, Lia Macha. The warrior fell to his knees and cried over this great loss. And so fell Lia Macha, the King of the horses.

The same events occur on the third attempt, but this time, the Satirist, or Calatan's third son, threatened to satirize Cú Chulainn's family if he didn't give him a spear. Cú Chulainn said, "Never let it be said that Cú Chulainn brought dishonor to his family," and smote the Satirist in the head with the spear. Lugaid Cu Roi drew his spear one last time and aimed it squarely at Cu Chulainn. The spear struck Cú Chulainn this time, and his intestines were sprayed out. However, he refused to give up and was still upright.

He had just enough power to crawl to a neighboring lake and gulp some water. Lugaid and his companions remained on the sidelines, fearful that Cu Chulainn had more might than he displayed. However, he was nearing the end of his life, and Cu Chulainn was aware of it. But he didn't want to die like an animal in the dirt. As a result, he gathered his remaining power and crawled to a big stone. He chained himself to the stone and gripped his sword fiercely, despite having little energy left in his body. As he stood there taking his last breaths, a raven came and tripped over his intestines; seeing this, Cú Chulainn laughed and died with that laugh in his mouth.

His opponents were unsure if he was really dead for 3 days after he died and were afraid to approach him in case he was still alive and waiting. Finally, at the end of the third day, Morrigan transformed into a raven and perched on Cu Chulainn's shoulder to announce his death to his enemies. Lugaid Cu Roi intended to steal C Chulainn's sword as a trophy as Cu Chulainn's foes approached his dead body, but he couldn't dislodge the sword from Cu Chulainn's grip. He pulled a knife and sliced Cu Chulainn's hand to free the sword, but the sword dropped and cut off Lugaid's hand.

One of Cú Chulainn's closest friends in arms, Conall Cernach, and he had taken a vow with each other to avenge the death of the one who fell before the other. When Conall Cernach heard about Cú Chulainn's death, he set out to avenge his brother and friend. Conall pursued Lugaid on horseback, and Lugaid, already having lost one hand, was weakened and couldn't run any further. Conall quickly catches up to Lugaid and challenges him to a fight. To make it fair, Conall ties one hand behind his back. However, neither of them comes close to winning the fight until Conall's horse takes a bite out of Lugaid's side. Conall then kills Lugaid and avenges Cú Chulainn.

Chapter 10

Da Derga's Hostel and the Importance of Keeping a Promise

Togail Bruidne Dá Derga, which translates into "The Destruction of Da Derga's Hostel," is among the most significant Irish tales in history. This legend belongs to the Ulster Cycle, which is a structure consisting of Ulaid Sagas and medieval Irish legends that revolve around heroic figures. *The Destruction of Da Derga's Hostel* survived, even after three editorial revisions during Old and Middle Ireland. This tale is part of the Book of Dun Cow. It tells the life story of Conaire Mor, Eterscél Mór's son, from his birth to when his enemies murdered him at da Derga's hostel after he broke a vow known as the geasa. Conaire Mor is one of Ireland's legendary High Kings.

Da Derga's Hostel is a very interesting story that keeps all the elements of the culture's oral storytelling. It gives a lot of insight into the people's beliefs about the essence of life, morals, and values.

The Ulster Cycle

The Ulster Cycle is a book of tales written during the time of Conchobar mac Nessa's reign. This King was the ruler of Ulaid, which was made up of a number of Gaelic Kingdoms located on the northeastern island during the Middle Ages. Cu Chulainn, who was Conshobar's nephew, is the most significant heroic figure in this cycle. There was a great deal of discord between the people of the Ulaid and those of the Connachta, a group of Irish dynasties led by queen Medb and Ailill, her husband. The conflict also often extended to include Fergus mac Roich, an exiled former king of the Ulaid, and the queen's ally. *Táin Bó Cúailnge, or the Cattle Raid of*

Cooley, which you can probably recall from the previous chapters, is the longest and most influential tale of the Ulster Cycle.

While Da Derga's Hostel is a rather serious story that teaches valuable life lessons and incorporates supernatural elements, along with day-to-day human challenges, struggles, traits, and nature, there are still some comedic conversations and incidents throughout the story. Reading Da Derga's Hostel, you'll get to learn all about Etain, the Celtic goddess who is known as the "Shining One," Eochaid, her mortal husband and Ireland's High King, and their successors, most notably, Conaire Mór, the legendary High King of Ireland.

This chapter tells the tale of Da Derga's Hostel and how it teaches the importance of keeping promises.

Da Derga's Hostel

The town of Ulster reached its peak popularity when it came to affluence and prosperity during the time following the rule of labroid the Voyager. All the stories and tales told at this time revolve around heroic triumphs and romantic escapades. This legend covers the tale of Conaire the Great, Tara's next King. It goes without saying that you'll come across a great deal of the customary fairy lore as you read on. This story supposedly takes place around 40 years prior to Jesus Christ's birth.

The tale begins with Eochaid the Constant Sighing, who was the King of Erin, riding over the vast plains of the King of the fairies, Longford. As he rode past Midir's fairy dwelling with his followers, he noticed a maiden who came from the mounds of the fairy standing beside a well. She was using a silver brush decorated with gold to brush her hair. She washed four golden birds in a silver basin with rims adorned with small purple gems. The lady was exceptionally beautiful and had gentle, irresistible eyes.

Bewitched by her beauty, Eochaid sent one of his men to ask her for her name. He was determined to seek her out as his wife. The maiden, who had introduced herself as Etain, explained that she was Etar's, the King of the fairy cavalcade daughter. She's lived there for 20 years, ever since her birth. Etain went on about how the fairy nobles and royals have been pursuing her even though she never returned their interest. She told Eochaid that her lack of interest in other men came from the profound love she'd developed for him while growing up through the tales of his grandeur and heroism she had heard as a child. Even though she had never seen him until that moment, she still felt like she knew him from afar.

Eochaid was over the moon and decided to marry her. He loved her deeply, and they had a daughter together. This girl grew up and married the King of Ulad, Cormac, and gave birth to one girl. Cormac, however, was incredibly angry because he wished for a son. Tragically, Cormac took out all his anger on his wife and daughter. He deprived the mother of her child and gave the baby away to two slaves so they could throw her into a pit. Seeing the newborn smile and laugh just as they were about to cast her away, the slaves couldn't bring themselves to do this to her. Instead, they took her home and decided to bring her up themselves.

Afraid of how the King would react if he found out that they disobeyed him and spared her life, they shut the girl in a wickerwork house when she grew up. The place was without a door and had but one window open to the sky.

One day, when the servants of Eterscel the King were out searching for food, they thought they would find corn hidden inside the house. So, they climbed up and looked down through the window to find the beautiful maiden trapped inside the hut with no way out. The servants rushed to tell the King about their interesting find, and so he sent out to fetch her so he could make her his wife.

The couple had a son named Conaire, who they sent to the Plain of Liffey so he could be brought up with his foster brothers. At some point, a group of soothsayers foretold that a young beardless boy who carried a sling and a stone would approach Tara and be chosen, King. Their prophecy came true when Conaire took over Erin after his father died.

Conaire's reign was very peaceful and prosperous, where trade and crops were abundant. He ordered them to leave and go disturb the men of Alba, which was Scotland at the time, instead. While they agreed to do that, it wasn't out of the goodness of their hearts. They were rather plotting to side with the King of Britain and together to take revenge on Conaire later.

Shortly after, Conaire heard of his brothers' successful attempts at instigating a war in Munster. The bearer of the news also explained that peace would never be achieved unless Conaire himself arrived to make peace between the parties. The King went to them, spending five nights with each, and made peace between them, although he knew it was dangerous to stand up to his brothers. Despite his ability to put the conflict to rest for some time, the war still went forward before Conaire even got the chance to arrive at Tara.

When Conaire asked his men about what was happening, they explained that people had broken the King's laws, destroyed them, and burned them up in flames. At that moment, Conaire and his men felt especially worried, considering that there was no way in which they could safely return to Tara. Since the northern area was blocked, they moved south toward the sea. When the King asked his men if they knew a place where they could spend the night, Mac Cecht, one of his best men, proclaimed that in the past, men had fought over who had the privilege of hosting a king, but now, its Conaire who's searching avidly for a guest house to take him up. Conaire said that with the passing of good times, so goes good judgment. He explained that he had a friend who lived in this country, but he didn't know the way to his house. Mac Cecht then asked for his name, and the King said that he was called "*De Derga of Leinster.*"

Conaire was positive that his friend would host him and his men for the night, as he had asked him for a favor not long before. The King said that not only did he give him the gift he asked for, but he would also do it again if De Derga came again and asked something of him. Mac Cecht said that he remembered the house and explained that the road they traveled was on the way to the house.

Da Derga's place is huge. It comes with seven doorways and bedrooms. Two doors were separating each bedroom from the one next to it. Mac Cecht said that if they wind up spending the night there, he will prepare a fire for the host.

Three Red Men riding red steeds came from the fairy mounds and rode past them as they set out toward the horse. The steeds appeared to be alive even though they weren't. Conaire's men tried calling onto those beings. However, they didn't budge, which prompted Conaire's son to ride off after them. Even though he was galloping at full speed, the boy failed to keep up with their speed. Though they disregarded Conaire and his men, the peculiar men sang a song as they approached the house of De Derga.

The men sang about the tired steeds they rode that had come from the fairy mounds of Donn Tetscorach. Their song warned about the end of life and looming destruction. They even made allusions to crows, ravens, and the wetted edge of the sword. Upon their arrival, the men tied their horses to the doors of the house and sat inside.

Conaire, his men, and the host immediately sensed that something bad would happen when they saw the three Red Men of the fairy mound coming up right before them. Everyone realized they were there to side with Conaire's enemies to take revenge. All those years had passed by, yet no one in the fairy realm had forgiven Etain for deciding to marry a mortal prince. They were also very aware that Conaire was a product of fairy birth. In short, he was the grandson of Etain's daughter. So, when Conaire caught sight of the men, he immediately knew that evil was on its way.

At that time, the foster brothers' sea fleet had gathered together with the British prince, Ingcel the One-eyed, arrived in Ireland once more, having ravaged Britain and Scotland. There were three fleets of fifty boats each. They had their sails furled and stayed beneath the Hill of Howth. The fleet sent two men of a good range of sight and hearing to the top of the hill. This way, they could keep an eye on Conaire and his men and find out where they went. The fleet noticed that they moved in the direction of De Derga's house and hoisted the sails. There were 5000men in total who sailed towards the shore. When they arrived, they moved quickly up the land and ended up somewhere not far below the hostel of Da Derga.

Conaire and his men entered the hostel before the sailors started to sneakily march up in the dark of the night. They covered the entire grounds surrounding the house. Each of the men had picked up a stone from the beach on their way up so they could build a cairn. This way, they were ready to destroy the building whenever they needed to. They made sure to set the cairn far away from the house so no one would accidentally catch a glimpse of it. While they watched the firelight and the men getting ready for demolition, some of the foster brothers had started to doubt their plan.

They felt guilty and prayed that the King would not spend the night at the hostel. In the end, his reign was peaceful and prosperous. He also had good and effective laws in place, they thought. Moreover, some hostages sought peace during their stay. Not to mention how young the King was, making it a pity to murder or destroy him. Sadly, the One-eyed British prince was still determined to go on with the plan either way. Ingcel was already spying on the house, directing his focused gaze right between his chariot's wheel so he could find out if Conaire was really inside the hostel.

The British royal declared that he would attack the house regardless of Conaire's presence, as he was determined to make the fine hostel his own. He believed that it was his right to raid it and take its spoils for his rights. None of the foster brothers disagreed with his plans. One of them even said that the decision lay in Ingcel's hands.

It was customary for the raiders to take a stone from the cairn upon their return. The number of stones left determined those who had fallen in battle. Ingcel then commanded that all men form a line and march up to the hostel to surround it.

Hearing the commotion from inside, Connaire demanded that everyone stay silent so he could make out what the noise was all about. One of the guards informed him that it was the sound of a fleet right outside the hostel. Conaire believed he had enough men to fight back., so he quickly gathered his men and his weapons together with his host and marched out of the house to face the fleet. Six hundred were killed at Conaire's charge. The fleet flung fire into the house three times, which were all put out.

At one point during the battle, Conaire was overcome by extreme thirst, and so he asked for a drink from his men. Little did he know that all the water and other liquids that were in the hostel had been used to put out the fire. The men also informed him that the Dodder River, the only body of water near the house, had also dried up. Then, Mac Cecht, one of Conaire's greatest and bravest men, seized the King's golden cup and fiercely charged through the army and out of the hostel with his spear in his hand.

He searched all the nearby and faraway lands for a lake or a river from which he could fill up his King's cup and quench his thirst. Even then, he was out of luck. A terrible drought had overtaken the nation, drying up all the rivers. He had nearly given up when he saw a wild duck come out of a pool that hid behind the trees in the distance. Mac Cecht made his way over and knelt down to fill up the cup. He was on his way back to the hostel just as the dawn had started to break.

Just as he turned toward the house, Mac Cecht saw Conaire's head flying off after being struck by one of the foster brothers. The King was too tired and too thirsty to fight him back. The angry Mac Cecht struck off an enemy's head and started throwing one stone after the other at the person running away with Conaire's head. Disappointed with his failure, Mac Cecht poured the water over the King's body before carrying it back to Tara so he could bury it. The good soldier then traveled to his homeland to recover from his injuries. Some believe that Ingcel went back to Alba, where he was named the kingdom's ruler, while others suggest that Mac Cecht and Conall destroyed the fleet the following morning and burnt all the ships to avenge Conaire.

Conclusion

Celtic mythology has had several legendary gods and heroes throughout history. Whether it's the stories of the Ulster cycle or the King's cycle, legendary heroism is the common theme among them all. Interestingly, Celtic mythology covers how the gods, immortal settlers, and humans interacted. Filled with Druid magic, fairies, beasts of all sorts, supernatural powers, and tragic endings, the world of Celtic mythology is full of color and adventure.

Today, most of Ireland's festivals are based on many of these rich, historical adventures featuring various gods and warriors. Even the concept of the mystical Otherworld isn't taken lightly in modern Irish culture. The early immortal settlers set the base of these adventures, and the brave warriors of each cycle helped fulfill them. The most prominent stories took place in Ulster, during the Ulster cycle. While there was no shortage of legendary warriors in Ulaid, the most popular one being Cú Chulainn, the Fenian cycle that followed had a much more prominent selection of warriors.

While there are many heroes talked about in Celtic mythology, the many tales of Fionn mac Cumhaill and Cú Chulainn dominate the rest of the legendary heroes. The many adventures of Fionn mac

Cumhaill make other stories pale in comparison. Whereas Cú Chulainn has also dominated most of the Ulster cycle, being the strongest and bravest warrior of the Ulaid. However, the death of Cú Chulainn was indeed a tragedy for all of Ulster. Another such tragedy was Deirdre's tale of sorrows, which, although it cannot be compared with Cú Chulainn's heroic battle story, has a tragic ending of its own.

The legend of Tir Na N-Óg in Celtic mythology is another great subject of interest for many readers. While some people believe it to be some sort of Otherworld with mystical creatures, others consider it to be mainly a fairyland. The Celtic Otherworld and the real world are supposedly in the same location, only in different dimensions. This concept certainly makes it more interesting for many people, even today.

Thank you for buying and reading/listening to our book. If you found this book useful/helpful please take a few minutes and leave a review on Amazon.com or Audible.com (if you bought the audio version).

References

Forsyth, S. (n.d.). Legends of Celtic mythology. Celtic-Weddingrings.Com. Retrieved from https://www.celtic-weddingrings.com/celtic-resources/legends-of-celtic-mythology

MacCulloch, J. A. (2017). Celtic Mythology. Andesite Press.

Why children should read mythology. (2018, February 27). The Curious Reader. https://www.thecuriousreader.in/essays/children-read-mythology/

Badnjarevic, D. (2021, January 12). 15 major Celtic Gods and Goddesses (you need to know about). The Irish Road Trip. https://www.theirishroadtrip.com/celtic-gods-and-goddesses/

Celtic culture - Cernunnos, the antlered god of power and blessing. (n.d.). Celticjewelry.Com. Retrieved from https://www.celticjewelry.com/celtic-culture/cernunnos

ConnollyCove. (2019, April 1). Morrigan: The fearless Celtic Goddess of War. ConnollyCove. https://www.connollycove.com/morrigan-goddess-of-war/

Lugh, master of skills. (2013, June 16). The Celtic Journey. https://thecelticjourney.wordpress.com/2013/06/16/lugh-master-of-skills/

Mandal, D. (2018, July 2). 15 ancient Celtic gods and goddesses you should know about. Realm of History. https://www.realmofhistory.com/2018/07/02/ancient-celtic-gods-goddesses-facts/

Mythologies, B. (2014, June 5). Midir. Bard Mythologies. https://bardmythologies.com/midir/

NicGriogha, B. (n.d.). Mythical Ireland. Mythical Ireland | New Light on the Ancient Past. Retrieved from https://mythicalireland.com/myths-and-legends/brigid-bright-goddess-of-the-gael/

No title. (n.d.). Com.Eg. Retrieved from https://www.twinkl.com.eg/teaching-wiki/irish-celtic-gods-and-goddesses

O'Hara, K. (2020, April 21). The Morrigan: The story of the fiercest goddess in Irish myth. The Irish Road Trip. https://www.theirishroadtrip.com/the-morrigan/

Smit, J. L. (2020, April 20). Celtic gods and goddesses: Exploring the pantheon and mythology of the ancient Celts. History Cooperative. https://historycooperative.org/celtic-gods-and-goddesses-celtic-pantheon/

The most important Celtic gods and goddesses. (n.d.). Sky HISTORY TV Channel. Retrieved from https://www.history.co.uk/articles/druid-deities-the-most-important-celtic-gods-and-goddesses

Top gods and goddesses from Celtic mythology. (2021, December 30). IrishCentral.Com. https://www.irishcentral.com/roots/history/celtic-mythology-gods-goddesses

West, B. (2020, January 29). Eriu :: A great goddess of the feminine Trinity of ancient Ireland. Projeda. http://www.projectglobalawakening.com/eriu/

Wigington, P. (n.d.-a). Brighid, the hearth goddess of Ireland. Learn Religions. Retrieved from https://www.learnreligions.com/brighid-hearth-goddess-of-ireland-2561958

Wigington, P. (n.d.-b). The Dagda, the father god of Ireland. Learn Religions. Retrieved from https://www.learnreligions.com/the-dagda-father-god-of-ireland-2561706

Wigington, P. (n.d.-c). The legend of lugh, the Celtic craftsman god. Learn Religions. Retrieved from https://www.learnreligions.com/lugh-master-of-skills-2561970

Wigington, P. (n.d.-d). The Morrighan. Learn Religions. Retrieved from https://www.learnreligions.com/the-morrighan-of-ireland-2561971

Wright, G. (2020a, August 16). Brigid. Mythopedia. https://mythopedia.com/topics/brigid

Wright, G. (2020b, August 16). Danu. Mythopedia. https://mythopedia.com/topics/danu

Badnjarevic, D. (2021, January 12). 31 Irish mythological creatures (tales told by an Irishman). The Irish Road Trip. https://www.theirishroadtrip.com/irish-mythological-creatures/

Bard, D. (2019, December 27). The gift of the Four Treasures. The Highland Bard. https://www.morgynbard.com/post/the-gift-of-the-four-treasures

Evans, Z. t. (n.d.). Exploring the Otherworld of the Celts. Folklorethursday.Com. Retrieved from https://folklorethursday.com/legends/exploring-the-otherworld-of-the-celts/

Fomorian (mythology). (n.d.). Villains Wiki. Retrieved from https://villains.fandom.com/wiki/Fomorian_(mythology)

Irish folklore. (2016, April 12). Lullymore Heritage And Discovery Park | Leading Visitor Attraction | Pet Farm | School Tours | Crazy Golf | Train Trips. https://www.lullymoreheritagepark.com/fairy-village-lone-bush-folklore/

O'Hara, K. (2020, April 16). The Fianna: The legend as told by an Irishman (2020 update). The Irish Road Trip. https://www.theirishroadtrip.com/the-fianna/

O'Hara, K. (2021, January 6). Fir Bolg: The Story of Irish Kings that were once Greek Slaves. The Irish Road Trip. https://www.theirishroadtrip.com/fir-bolg/

The Editors of Encyclopedia Britannica. (2016). Milesians. In Encyclopedia Britannica.

The true story behind 'the Fianna.' (n.d.). Irishimbasbooks.Com. Retrieved from https://irishimbasbooks.com/the-true-story-behind-the-fianna/

Where do myths, legends, and folktales come from? (n.d.). Ox.Ac.Uk. Retrieved from https://www.torch.ox.ac.uk/article/where-do-myths-legends-and-folktales-come-from

Cove, C. (2018, February 21). The whole interesting history of the Tuatha de Danann: Ireland's most ancient race. ConnollyCove. https://www.connollycove.com/tuatha-de-danann/

Donnchadha, P. M. (2012, February 21). The Fir Bolg & the third invasion of Ireland. Your Irish Culture. https://www.yourirish.com/folklore/third-invasion-of-ireland

Fir bolg: An ancient people of Irish mythology. (2021, September 29). MythBank. https://mythbank.com/fir-bolg/

Mythologies, B. (2014a, May 6). Nuadhu of the silver arm. Bard Mythologies. https://bardmythologies.com/nuadhu-of-the-silver-arm/

Mythologies, B. (2014b, June 5). Breas. Bard Mythologies. https://bardmythologies.com/breas/

Mythologies, B. (2014c, June 5). Lugh. Bard Mythologies. https://bardmythologies.com/lugh/

Perkins, M. (n.d.). Irish mythology: History and legacy. ThoughtCo. Retrieved from https://www.thoughtco.com/irish-mythology-4768762

solsdottir. (2018, July 18). Nuada: the King with the silver arm. We Are Star Stuff. https://earthandstarryheaven.com/2018/07/18/nuada/

The Battle of Magh Tuireadh (literature). (n.d.). TV Tropes. Retrieved from https://tvtropes.org/pmwiki/pmwiki.php/Literature/TheBattl eOfMaghTuireadh

Wright, G. (2020, August 16). Nuada. Mythopedia. https://mythopedia.com/topics/nuada

Evslin, B. (2012). The Green hero: Early adventures of Finn McCool. Open Road Media Teen & Tween.

Finn McCool Marketing. (2019, November 6). Finn McCool Marketing. https://www.finn-mccool.co.uk/irish-mythology/the-legend-of-finn-mccool/

Irish Kids Irish Children's Stories Irish culture and customs - World Cultures European. (n.d.). Irishcultureandcustoms.Com. Retrieved from https://www.irishcultureandcustoms.com/1Kids/StoryofSad hbh.html

The Story of Finn Children's Stories Irish culture and customs - World Cultures European. (n.d.). Irishcultureandcustoms.Com. Retrieved from https://www.irishcultureandcustoms.com/1Kids/FinnAillen. html

Fionn and the Fianna. (n.d.). Irelandsmythsandlegends.Com.
    Retrieved from
    http://www.irelandsmythsandlegends.com/fionn-and-the-
    fianna

Salmon of Knowledge, Kids Stories Irish culture, and customs -
    World Cultures European. (n.d.).
    Irishcultureandcustoms.Com. Retrieved from
    http://www.irishcultureandcustoms.com/1Kids/Salmon.html

Mythologies, B. (2014, June 11). Diarmuid and Gráinne. Bard
    Mythologies. https://bardmythologies.com/diarmuid-and-
    grainne/

Donnchadha, P. M. (2016, October 20). Deirdre of the Sorrows.
    Your Irish Culture.
    https://www.yourirish.com/folklore/deirdre-of-the-sorrows

Mythologies, B. (2014, June 11). Deirdre of the sorrows. Bard
    Mythologies. https://bardmythologies.com/deirdre-of-the-
    sorrows/

Synge, J. M. (2017). Deirdre of the sorrows. Createspace
    Independent Publishing Platform.

Synge, John Millington. (2015). Deirdre of the sorrows: A play -
    scholar's choice edition. Scholar's Choice.

The Story of Deirdre - Irish fairy story. (2020, September 3).
    Ireland Calling. https://ireland-calling.com/story-of-deirdre/

The debility of the ulstermen. (n.d.). Archive.Org. Retrieved from
   https://web.archive.org/web/20131226141502/http://www.
   maryjones.us/ctexts/debility.html

The Editors of Encyclopedia Britannica. (2007). The Cattle Raid of
   Cooley. In Encyclopedia Britannica.

The Táin (The Cattle Raid of Cooley). (n.d.). Encyclopedia.Com.
   Retrieved from https://www.encyclopedia.com/arts/culture-
   magazines/tain-cattle-raid-cooley

T'in B' C'ailnge: The Cattle Raid of Cooley. (n.d.).
   Askaboutireland.Ie. Retrieved from
   https://www.askaboutireland.ie/learning-zone/primary-
   students/looking-at-places/louth/tain-bo-cuailnge-the-catt/

Folklore, I., & Traditions. (2019, July 26). The evolution of the
   Irish Otherworld. Ireland's Folklore and Traditions.
   https://irishfolklore.wordpress.com/2019/07/26/the-
   evolution-of-the-irish-otherworld/

The Fairy-Faith in Celtic Countries: The recorded Fairy-Faith:
   Chapter VI. Celtic Otherworld. (n.d.). Sacred-Texts.Com.
   Retrieved from https://www.sacred-
   texts.com/neu/celt/ffcc/ffcc260.htm

The legend of tir Na nog the land of youth. (n.d.).
   Horsesoftirnanog.Org. Retrieved from
   http://www.horsesoftirnanog.org/about/the-legend/

O'Halloran, S. (2021, December 5). The ancient Irish myth
   Children of Lir, the basis for Swan Lake. IrishCentral.Com;
   IrishCentral. https://www.irishcentral.com/roots/irish-myth-
   children-lir-swan-lake

Oíde cloinne Lir = The fate of the children of Lir : O'Duffy,
Richard J., ed : Free Download, Borrow, and Streaming :
(n.d.). Internet Archive. Retrieved from
https://archive.org/details/oieloinnelirfate00oduf

Soranescu, A. (2015a). The children of lir: An Irish legend. Xlibris.

Soranescu, A. (2015b). The children of lir: An Irish legend. Xlibris.

Cú roí (deity). (n.d.). Talabhanu Wiki. Retrieved from
https://talabhanu.fandom.com/wiki/C%C3%BA_Ro%C3%
AD_(Deity)

Miller, F. P., Vandome, A. F., & McBrewster, J. (Eds.). (2010a).
Cu Chulainn. Alphascript Publishing.

Mythologies, B. (2014, May 6). The death of Cuchulainn. Bard
Mythologies. https://bardmythologies.com/the-death-of-
cuchulainn/

No title. (n.d.). Academickids.Com. Retrieved from
https://academickids.com/encyclopedia/index.php/Curoi_ma
c_Daire

Williams, A. (2020, August 16). Cu Chulainn. Mythopedia.
https://mythopedia.com/topics/cu-chulainn

Pagan Ireland by Eleanor Hull - The Destruction of Da Derga's
Hostel. (n.d.). Irishevents4u.Com. Retrieved from
http://www.irishevents4u.com/books/elenor-hull/pagen-
ireland/021.htm

Printed by BoD™in Norderstedt, Germany